T0194482

THE
KENOSIS
EPIDEMIC

WHAT IS THE COST OF TRUTH?

ALISTAIR J. WALKER

WESTBOW
PRESS®
A DIVISION OF THOMAS NELSON
& ZONDERVAN

This is a work of fiction. All of the characters, names, incidents, organizations, and dialogue in this novel are either the products of the author's imagination or are used fictitiously.

WestBow Press books may be ordered through booksellers or by contacting:

WestBow Press
A Division of Thomas Nelson & Zondervan
1663 Liberty Drive
Bloomington, IN 47403
www.westbowpress.com
1 (866) 928-1240

Because of the dynamic nature of the Internet, any web addresses or links contained in this book may have changed since publication and may no longer be valid. The views expressed in this work are solely those of the author and do not necessarily reflect the views of the publisher, and the publisher hereby disclaims any responsibility for them.

Any people depicted in stock imagery provided by Getty Images are models, and such images are being used for illustrative purposes only. Certain stock imagery © Getty Images.

ISBN: 978-1-9736-2517-9 (sc)
ISBN: 978-1-9736-2518-6 (hc)
ISBN: 978-1-9736-2516-2 (e)

Library of Congress Control Number: 2018904172

Print information available on the last page.

WestBow Press rev. date: 10/25/2018

In memory of Pastor Phil Huber

My friend Phil Huber was kind enough the read my manuscript and give me his opinions, feedback, and a recommendation. I contacted pastor Phil because I trusted Him. Trusted him to give a thorough, honest and complete assessment of the book and its message. He sent me a wonderful letter full of kindness and praise for my work.

Unfortunately earlier this year, just shy of his forty-fifth birthday, Pastor Phil passed away. Leaving a wonderful wife and family heartbroken. Upon receiving the news of his passing I wondered if my book was the last one he read. It made me think the gravity of that concept. What if something you wrote or said was going to be the last thing someone hears or reads. Is it kind? Did it help? Was it uplifting to God?

Phil left that kind of legacy. Filling his daily Facebook posts with encouraging Bible verses and loving words for those who needed it. Laying a much needed welcome mat at the door of the church for tired and weary souls.

Thank you Phil for a life that made a difference.
Pastor Phil, Husband Phil, Father Phil....My friend Phil Huber.
Your legacy lives on...

Thank you Jen Huber and family for allowing me this dedication during a very difficult time.

God be with you.

CHAPTER 1

There was a loud, piercing screech, and I woke suddenly to the sound of wheels hitting the tarmac as the plane touched down and skidded abruptly to a stop. The icy sleet on my face as the storm hammered down reminded me it was going to be a cold winter. It was the best of times; it was the worst of times. These are all great ways to start a story – sharp, dramatic, in your face. They allow you to know that things are about to happen, and that you need to pay attention because an epic story is about to unfurl before you.

But for me, it wasn't that way. There was no loud screech. It wasn't icy outside or scorching hot; it was a pleasant, ordinary day. This isn't some bittersweet story that tells you times were good even when times were bad. It's a story about me, an ordinary man with an ordinary life – very ordinary, in fact. I'm not a hero, at least not one with a cape or a badge, one they make movies about, or one with chiselled good looks and snappy catchphrases. I am, in fact, the very definition of plain and uninteresting.

My name is Dr David Amiasaf. I run a small general practice with my brother just outside of Darlington in County Durham, England. It's a lovely little nook of Britain if I do say so myself. The streets are clean, and the people are decent. Although the weather doesn't always cooperate with a planned day out, one gets used to it. One might say I live in an almost perfect world. Thanks to the governmental and para-governmental organizations, after centuries of petty squabbling, governments started to listen to one another and work together for the greater good. They united almost all the nations with common goals. They then set out to eliminate all waste and global poisoning. No more wasting fuel; we all have a monthly allotment. No unwanted children; the designed family council approves all pregnancies, and any accidents are immediately terminated. No more greedy people; we are all allowed to earn our own money within reason, but if our accounts go over, the government takes the excess and uses it for much-needed social programs. No more waste; everything is immediately recycled, and everything has an energy cell, so whether we are walking or riding a bike, we are powering energy cells for use in your home. It comes in handy if we get close to using up our monthly energy allowance.

Since the global union, we are all far more educated and enlightened, and we push forward as a worldwide population that cares more about the collective than the individual. It's as near a perfect world as one could wish for. So what exactly is my story? Is my story one of luck, fate, or some mystical divine hand of almighty God? I guess it depends on what one believes, and I never much cared for luck or divine inspiration. I simply live my life.

CHAPTER 2

As a doctor, I have seen a lot of things happen over the years. Since I was a child, technology has made leaps and bounds in everything, including medicine. I mean huge leaps and bounds, not mere hops. In life, we see great things happen, we marvel for a moment or so, and then we quickly get back to life. I suppose we have gotten used to technology and miracles being run-of-the-mill, so we just don't marvel quite the way we used to. In fact, we just expect these miracles to be delivered on a regular basis. But in reality, no major diseases are being cured, and nothing medically important has happened since the world unified and went completely digital – up until about eight years ago.

Miles McTarvish, a research scientist from Northern Ireland, was working at his lab in Wrexham, Wales, when he changed the face of the medical world as we know it. He invented empathetic medicine. In short, Dr McTarvish invented a machine that picked up all the feelings of one individual and transferred them into another. By hooking electrodes to the doctor and the patient, the doctor could transfer exactly what the patient was feeling into himself. The doctor could then feel the aches, pains, and symptoms firsthand; quickly diagnose the patient; and dispense the appropriate treatment. It took all the guesswork out of modern medicine.

Like a bang, this new form of treating patients exploded and changed the world as we knew it. Although we cannot cure any more diseases than we could a few years ago, people coming into the waiting rooms are diagnosed, treated, and released without any need for wondering or second opinions. Immediately these machines were sent to all universities, enabling medical students to learn firsthand what every disease felt like. When a patient came into their offices or hospitals, doctors would already know what it felt like to have kidney stones, a torn muscle, or even a brain tumour, and they could diagnose immediately. In order to keep an active license, all doctors with fewer than five years to go before retirement – myself included, because I was very much in the prime of my medical life – had to go back to medical school and be subjected to the same empathetic treatments as the students.

Modern medicine can be summarized thusly: quick diagnosis, immediate medicine, and relief. Nobody suffered very long, except for those with the few diseases we haven't cured yet. Things like cancer are not cured, though it is now detected sooner, giving patients a better chance of survival. However, there are still things that are mysteries, like headaches and colds.

Then there was the dreaded kenosis epidemic that happened a few years back. Almost everybody suffered from that. It was an epidemic that spread like wildfire about five years ago. We haven't even determined where it came from or how it started. It affected the central nervous system, causing headaches, nausea, blurred vision, loss of balance, and more. Modern medicine came out with a pill for the symptoms. Although it didn't cure the disease, as long as we all took our pills, everybody was fine. Or so we thought.

CHAPTER 3

My story begins after a long work stretch with a heavy patient load. I was very much overworked, tired, and apparently very irritable, as I was told by my family and co-workers. I planned a much-needed holiday. I found us a holiday home in Kent for the week. My wife, our two kids, and I were heading out one evening just after work. The bags were packed, the house was locked, and the dog was with my parents. My brother was going to be taking care of the practice while I was gone, and it was finally time for some long overdue rest and relaxation.

We loaded up that evening after the usual what-are-we-forgetting panic attack everyone experiences right before leaving on holiday. I programmed the car's satellite navigation chauffeur and relaxed with the family as the car steadily headed towards our destination. I always enjoyed the drive because the scenery was very beautiful along the coast roads. The car drove through the night as we slept; it didn't take too long, and soon we arrived at the holiday home. This one was in a gated community of about ten holiday homes with a community pool in the middle that everybody shared. It was a short drive to the beach, shops, and restaurants. I could tell we were going to enjoy this very much, and I already started to relax. We unpacked the vehicle, and I took the bags to the door and scanned in as the ladies got back into the car and headed to the market for food. I suggested that they get onto the interweb and send in an order, but they insisted on going out to do a bit of exploring.

The first night was quiet and peaceful. The air down there was so fresh! The next morning, my blissful sleeping in was abruptly ended by the alarm on my personal communication device, which I'd forgotten to turn off. It woke me up at six as it did every day for work. I leaned over, fumbled around to turn it off, and went back to sleep. I was awakened again a few hours later at eight by Mrs Dumfries, a patient I had mistakenly given my mobile number to some years back. She had not wanted to talk to my brother – she wanted to talk to me, and only me. The kids were already up and ready to head to the pool, and I muted my communicator so Mrs Dumfries couldn't hear. I told my wife to go on to the pool without me, adding that I would do my best to pacify fussy Mrs Dumfries and be there in a moment. I explained to Mrs Dumfries as carefully as I could, using enough medical terms to make her think I was talking with her medical e-pad in my hand, that she wasn't going to die today. I quickly said goodbye and headed to the pool.

CHAPTER 4

My son, Jeremiah, was looking for a fight, and he wasn't going to take no for an answer. As quickly as I could, I grabbed him, threw him into the pool, and dove on top of him. We wrestled around, and then my daughter came over and jumped on my back. We swam for what seemed like hours, and then I got out and sat for a while, exhausted. The kids, with endless energy, swam for another few hours. "Come on, kids," I said. "This is the only night I'm doing this. I'm taking your mum and you kiddies out to a fine meal, so let's get going. There's a pub just around the corner, or so I was told by the house owner."

We walked back to the house, and upon changing into my clothes, I looked down and discovered it truly was the best of times and the worst of times. I had jumped into the pool with my person communicator in my pocket. It had been submerged for several hours, so there was no doubt that it was ruined. However, something told me I wasn't going to die without it for a week, and the silence could be divine. Besides, I could get a new one as soon as we got back home to Darlington. I knew I could get one locally, but how often was I ever without that blasted noise box? Never! After this morning's holiday crashing by Mrs Dumfries, I was not about to rush to replace it.

I headed down to the living room, and we headed to the pub. It was a lovely meal and a lovely evening with the family. The kids even kept their squabbling to a minimum, which probably meant that my wife gave them a "Dad really needs to relax" lecture.

CHAPTER 5

We left the pub and headed back to the house to settle in. I made sure the kids took their medicine before they went to bed, and then the wife and I headed to our bed to sit and talk before we went to sleep.

"Love, hand me my pills when you are getting yours," I said.

"I didn't pack your pills," she said. "I thought you did."

"No," I said. "I thought *you* packed them. Well, that's the end of that. I'm going to die tonight, and it's all your fault. Are you happy now?"

"Don't be so dramatic," Rachael said. "You're not going to die. Though I did think you might drown earlier."

"I know," I replied. "When did that boy get so strong? Anyway, it doesn't matter. Everybody's pills are the same. I'll just take some of yours."

Taking somebody else's medicine was an inconvenience and was frowned upon because we were all allotted the same amount every month. When we ran out, we got an e-mail saying it was time to refill in a few days. We'd go down to the local chemist, and they'd scan us and give us our pills. Everything was neatly documented. At least, it was if one used a pin and chip, like my wife and I did. My dad still used money, and there was a lot of paperwork involved in that. We simply scanned the chip in our hands and put in our PIN to get our medicine. It was a lot easier than the way Dad did it, but I guessed he was set in his ways. All medicine could be received by post, if one desired, with the only exception being the medicine for the kenosis epidemic. That medicine had to be picked up in person.

Anyway, as long as I kept count of how many I took of Rachael's pills, I could give her that many back when I got home. I took a pill from Rachael and put it on the night stand. "I'll take it in a bit," I said.

Rachael gave me the "Just take it now" look and took hers. She sat on the bed next to me, we talked for a few minutes, and then she rolled over and went to sleep. I sat and watched a little television, which I never did back home because I didn't like to be tired the next morning for work. But there was no work for me tomorrow, and so I could indulge. Just my misfortune: a documentary on the North American sand flea. This was just the thing to take me to the land of nod.

"Come on! Come on! Let's go! Let's go swimming again."

Dad, come on! Let's go to the pool!"

I was awakened by the delightful sound of children obsessed with a swimming pool. "Okay, okay," I said. "I'm coming. Give me a minute. I was thinking about getting dressed and having a cuppa first, but obviously we'd better get into that ruddy pool before someone runs off with all the water. Big aquatic crime wave around these parts, I hear.

"Seriously, Dad?" they smugly replied. "We really want to go. Come on!"

Perhaps no one was stealing the pool water, but I did feel as though I had taken my fair share of the chlorine home in my eyes yesterday. "All right, you little hooligans. I'm coming."

CHAPTER 6

I reached for my wallet and my watch on the nightstand as Rachael got the kids ready and headed to the pool. "I'll be there in a second," I said. I reached across the nightstand, and there it was, larger than life: Rachael's pill she had given me last night. I'd forgotten to take it! It was disastrous if one forgot to take the medicine. As a doctor, I knew that better than anybody. But I *had* forgotten.

Strangely enough, I felt fine. Normally when people didn't take their pills, symptoms started quickly, usually within an hour. I hadn't had any symptoms; in fact, I felt fine. I felt great! I thought about it for a moment and then simply put it out of my mind. I didn't know what had happened, but I was on holiday. I could figure it out later. I headed to the pool, leaving the pill on the nightstand where I had placed it the night before.

We had another full day swimming in the pool, followed by a leisurely walk down to the beach. Then there was another brisk walk to the town for some wife-inspired bit of shopping. It was another nice, relaxing day on holiday, just like any other day and anybody else's life – except for me, because I'd had no pill. We got back to the house and settled in for a quiet evening. I picked up the pill and looked at it for a moment. Then I dropped it into the nightstand draw. Rachael handed me another pill, took hers, and left to give the kids theirs. I held mine in my hand and waited for everyone to go to bed. I walked to the bed, sat down, opened my hand, and stared at the pill. Then I quietly opened the nightstand drawer and put the pill in with the one from the night before. I looked at the draw, as if staring would prompt the answers to my many questions to come more quickly. The intense staring soon gave way to heavy eyelids, and after a few moments I faded.

The next morning came, and again I woke up refreshed and fine. Well, not fine, but great – really great. I felt better than the day before I think. I was puzzled. One more night had passed, and then another. On Friday, I sat down on the bed with Rachael and looked at her. She was going on about the wonderful weather, how perfect the week had been, and all the usual chatter that followed a nice holiday. I listened – well, sort of. I was trying to listen, but all I could really think about was, *How do I talk to her about this without alarming her?* I hadn't gotten hold of this myself yet. Was I cured? Did the medicine help me build an immunity? Was it a fluke that was temporary? I did not know, but I needed to confide in her, so I mustered up the courage.

CHAPTER 7

"Sweetheart, I want you to do me a favour," I said. "It's a big one – a very big one. Do you think you could find it within you to have some faith in me and do it?"

"Well, of course, love. I'll certainly try," she said. "What is it?"

I looked at her and froze. I wasn't sure how to phrase it. "Do you mind staying up late and watching a movie with me tonight?"

"Is that it?" she said. "That's not such a huge favour. I don't mind at all."

"Well, there's more," I muttered. "Don't take your medicine yet."

She looked at me and as expected, said, "I have to, dear. It's time."

"Just wait an hour. That's the favour: wait about an hour. All right? Then you can take it. I promise everything will be fine."

She looked at me a bit strangely, as if a million questions were racing through her mind, and then she agreed. We lay back and watched whatever was on – another boring documentary, I think. About forty-five minutes went by, and I thought to myself, *Everything is going to be fine.*

But everything wasn't fine. It seemed I was quite wrong with my hypothesis. After watching the movie for about an hour, the inevitable happened. Right on cue, she suddenly became sick. Dizziness, headache, nausea, and several other symptoms of the disease rushed upon her. I quickly scrambled to get her pill, and after fumbling with the lid, I got one out. She took it. Another hour went by, and after what must have seemed like an eternity, she lay her head in my lap to try to find some relief. Gradually, the symptoms faded. She was exhausted from the ordeal, and I was riddled with guilt for causing her pain – and even more so for treating her like some sort of laboratory testing animal. I stroked her hair and stared at her.

I didn't have the heart to tell her I hadn't been taking my pills all week; she would panic or worry, or both. No, there was no need to tell her right now. I was puzzled. A week without pills, and I was fine – but in just one hour without hers, she was sick, convulsing, dizzy, and ready to head to the nearest hospital. I kept thinking over and over, *One full week, and I'm fine. No, not simply fine – I'm great.* Once again my mind flooded with reasoning as to why. I was desperate to get to a conclusion, some sensible reason for this. I had taken my pills on time every day over the last five years. Had I built up an immunity to this crazy disease? Did prolonged use of the pill cure me? Was this to do with my sex? Perhaps only men built up an immunity? Should I tell anyone? It seemed I was cured. Was I a miracle person? Was there something in my blood that had killed the disease? Thousands of questions came to mind. Perhaps some tests of my blood when I got back would give me some answers.

The ride back was fun, and the view of the countryside occupied my mind, if only for a short while. We laughed and played games. We were a pretty close family. After some time, Rachael did ask why I'd made her go without her pill for an hour. I told her it was just me being a doctor, testing everything for science's sake. I stumbled clumsily though my explanation, but she believed me. I must have apologised a dozen times, and I knew there was no hiding the guilt on my face. She knew I felt badly and reassured me that I was forgiven.

CHAPTER 8

We arrived home safe and sound. Holidays seemed to take forever in coming but were over in a flash. We unpacked and sent the car to Jacob's for the dog. Saturday evening came, and I had to admit it was wonderful to be home.

"I'm glad to finally be back," I said.

"Me too," replied Rachael. "This was one of the strangest weeks we've ever spent."

"That's a peculiar thing to say. What exactly do you mean?" I enquired.

"Well … Didn't you notice how much more … Umm, well … Blimey, this isn't easy to put delicately. Never mind."

"How much more what?" I snapped. "It's clear that you have something to tell me, so tell me."

Rachael and I had a rule that went back to our first date at the tea shop around the corner from my mum and dad's old house. Smarmy, posh, and expensive tea shops were all the rage back then. Trendy flavoured teas and coffee sold at an exorbitant price. Then we all woke up one day and realized nothing was better than the original: a hot cup of Earl Grey was all anyone needed in the tea department. In a flash, the specialty shops were gone.

Anyway, the rule was that if we started to say something, then we must finish it, no matter what it was. Even if it was scary, mean, or hurtful, "never minds" and "forget its" were not allowed.

She started slowly and cautiously. "Well, you were more ...." obtuse."

"Obtuse?" I repeated, feeling puzzled. "Are you talking about me? I'm anything but obtuse. I'm Mr Flexible, Mr Easygoing, Mr Easy to Deal With. In fact, I'm thinking of changing my name to just that: Mr Easy to Deal With."

"Actually, sweetheart, it would be Dr Easy to Deal With," she rebutted.

"That's even better, isn't it? Dr Easy to Deal With it is."

"I think Dr Overly Dramatic fits better in this instance," she replied. "Anyway, perhaps obtuse is not the right word. I certainly didn't mean obtuse in a rude way. You were more direct. Yes, direct is a better word. More straightforward."

I sighed. "Direct? Well, if you say so, love. I'll settle for Dr Direct. Anyway, I plan to have a restful, peaceful, and extremely easygoing Sunday. Then tomorrow I'll deal with the grind of a noisy office and grumpy patients."

But how true those words were, and what a grind it turned out to be. Monday arrived, and it was every bit as bad as I had predicted. Patients didn't like substitutes, even if they already knew them. Dealing with the ailments of one body was a very personal experience. Patients want me and only me, not my assistant, not my coworker, and not even my brother. It didn't matter how many times they'd seen him around the office, or that he was a good doctor. They were my patients, and they wanted to see me.

My patients told me in detail how much they missed me. It was flattering and annoying at the same time. *Let me just finish my day,* I thought. But after that, it was off to get this in and out radio looked at, and then I had to go to the mobile store for a new phone. Then I'd head to the grocers for a loaf of bread and some wine. My parents were coming for dinner tonight, so I needed to move quickly. I didn't want to hear it if I was running late after a week off.

CHAPTER 9

Finally I was back home. I parked the car in its usual spot and went inside to greet everyone. The man at the radio store had taken a bit longer than I had anticipated fixing my radio, and so I did end up late after all. My parents were already inside.

"Hello, Dad," I said as I came through the door. "Hello, Mum. Give us a kiss. How are you two feeling these days?"

"We're fine, son. Stop being a doctor for a few moments," my mum replied.

"Not being a doctor, just being a son. C'mon, how's Dad's knees? Still giving him trouble?"

"They're okay," she said. "We walk around the block twice every evening."

"Lovely," I said. "All right, Rachael. Where's the food? I'm famished!"

"It's ready," she said. "You're late, remember?"

"Oh, of courses. Well, point me to the food!"

We went into the dining room for a lovely dinner. Naturally, Mum and Dad wanted to know all about our holiday. Rachael had prepared a lovely meal, as usual. Dinner was soon over, and so we adjourned to the living room for tea and biscuits and some nice conversation. "Can I give the kids fifty pounds each?" my dad said.

"Fifty pounds? I tell you what. You can give *me* fifty pounds, and I promise to spend it on useless old tat and bad food. That's the same as giving it to the kids."

"Come on," Dad said.

"Have they been down here giving you the sad eyes?" I asked.

"No, not at all. Nothing like that," he said. "I'm their grandpa, I've got the money, and I want to give it to them. I don't need a reason."

"Fair enough," I said. "It's hard to put up a resistance to an argument like that."

Dad pulled out his wallet and pulled out two fifty-pound notes.

"Paper money? Still? When are you guys going to move into the present?" Rachel said.

"You mean those dreadful chips they put in your hands? I'm sure one day I'll have to, but it seems too technical for me – a little too sterile. I like the feel of money. I like to look in my wallet and see money. Call me old-fashioned, but all these invisible pounds and dollars and euros floating around in some interweb terminal's brain doesn't seem real to me."

"You know we can go to any ATM and get cash anytime we want, with our chips," Rachael said. "Besides, I heard that in five years or so, they're going to make the chip mandatory and get rid of paper money altogether. You might as well do it now and give yourself time to get used to it."

"I'll do it when they make me," Dad said. "I know I have to do it. I just don't want to be pushed right now."

"Well, enough of this," I said. "Money is money. Doesn't matter where it comes from. It's insignificant as long as you get your pay cheque, right? Let's not fuss about it. Now, call these kids in here, and let Grandpa play the big shot."

The kids had no reluctant feelings about taking the money. In fact, they were quite expedient about snatching it up and tucking it into their pockets.

Rachael said, "Looks like I'm one hundred pounds richer come laundry time!" The kids paused at the bottom of the stairs.

"That's right," I said. "Better not leave it in your pockets, because once it's in the laundry room, it's hers. I lost a fifty that way years ago. Now I thoroughly check my pockets before releasing them to be washed." The kids scurried off, looking quite nervous.

"I thought your brother Jacob was going to be here tonight, David," Mum said.

I said, "He was supposed to be, but he had to work late. You know how it is when you are dedicated to your work. We take turns filing the reports, and tonight is Jacob's turn. It's only once a week. Besides, aren't we going to his house for Dad's birthday next weekend?"

"Oh!" Rachael burst out loudly. "You've spoiled the surprise!"

"What surprise?" Dad said. "Every year, we go to one of your houses for my birthday, and every year I'm supposed to act like I have no idea why. It's *my* birthday. I'm not that good an actor."

"See?" I smugly replied to Rachael. "He knows. He's very clever when he wants to be."

Mum quipped, "Funny. Your father says the same thing about you."

"And for good reason," I replied. "I am a doctor."

"Quite a cheeky one tonight," Mum added.

"See? I told you!" Rachael blurted out.

"Told him what?" Dad asked.

"Nothing of any consequence," I replied. "Rachael thinks I've been acting more assertively this last week. We're watching my sugar intake. Sleep well, you two."

CHAPTER 10

After my parents left, we settled the kids into their beds and then made our way towards our bedroom and a much-anticipated night's rest. I grabbed my medicine bottle, as I had so many thousands of times before. I twisted off the lid and put my pill into my hand to take it ... but I couldn't. I didn't see the need, so instead I stared at it. *Nine days,* I thought. *It's been going on nine days, I haven't had a pill, and I hadn't had a symptom. In fact I hadn't even had anything remotely close to resembling a symptom. I hadn't even had a headache.* As if that wasn't puzzling enough, I also had no withdrawal from coming off the medication so abruptly.

I put the pill back into the medicine bottle, grabbed the glass, and feigned taking it. "Good night, my love," I said. Rachael had already taken her pill and had gotten into bed. I lay back against my pillows, and Rachael snuggled up to me.

"Good night, love," she replied.

I dozed off into a fog, thinking of the day's activities and what I had to do tomorrow. My half planning gave way to restful sleep.

Suddenly I was awake, groggy, and disoriented. I knew I wasn't asleep that long – an hour, maybe. *I don't feel well,* I thought. I had an intensely throbbing head that wouldn't stop pounding; I could barely think. *I'm going to be sick. I have to get to the toilet.* I fell out of bed and scrambled to the bathroom. The headache was so intense now, pulsating behind my eyes. I could barely open my eyes. I was crawling on the bedroom floor, but by this time I was so dizzy, even that was becoming more of an impossibility.

I was halfway to the bathroom when my mind suddenly thought of my medicine. I quickly turned back and headed for my nightstand, fumbling around in the dark on the bedroom floor. The pain was miserable; it felt like the nightstand was a hundred miles away. After what seemed like an eternity, I found it. I grabbed the bottle and fumbled at the lid, clumsily at first but then angrily because I couldn't get the lid off. I paused and slowed down; this time it worked. The lid came off, and I got my pill out and swallowed it with no water. I fell back to the hard floor in anguish. I lay on the floor holding my temples for an hour or so, rocking back and forth as if it would ease the pain while trying to be as quiet as possible, so as not to wake Rachael – or throw up. After about an hour, the pain slowly subsided. *Wow. I never want to feel that again.* That was all I could think, over and over. I was physically drained. I didn't think I had the strength to pull myself up into bed. I had never been without my medicine before – not once since the epidemic had started five years ago. I had always taken my medicine on time, so until tonight, I had never experienced the physical and mental trauma of this horrible disease.

But it was over, and I felt better. In fact, I felt good again, though I was completely exhausted. The experience had taken everything out of me, but I was so happy that it was over, and I was ready for sleep. I crawled back over and pulled myself up into bed. It took me no time to fall asleep, and I slept soundly. I would wake the next morning and that would be it. That would be my tale, all finished. The story of a worldwide epidemic and the man who'd took over a week off from it. It was not an altogether great story, was it? I mean, I did say in the beginning that I was quite an ordinary bloke, nothing too noteworthy about me. I suppose this story has been anticlimactic for even the most mundane of people, and for that I am sorry. It was a minor mystery, as yet unsolved, as to why I'd gone nine days without my medicine and no symptoms, but now I had this attack.

One pill later, and all was well. If one had time, one might look into solving it. However, I didn't have the time. Life got in the way, and quite frankly, the next morning I simply didn't care. My life went back to normal, back to the way it was before, back to perfection. Until …

CHAPTER 11

Six weeks had gone by since my week off from the pills. All was well, and I was content to live with the mystery – or mysteries, I should say. The second mystery was why I'd been so obsessed with it that week. Rachael was right: I'd been driven that week. *Wait, she never said driven. She said direct.* But I was driven. I really wanted to know why I was fine, why my symptoms had vanished. At present, I didn't really care.

I was awakened from my daydream because my personal communicator was ringing. I answered it, and it as was Rachael.

"Are you going to work late?" she inquired.

"No, not that I know of," I said.

"Okay. Call me on the way home, please."

"Will do. Love you." I stared at my communicator for a minute. I didn't like it and missed my old one. I'd had that one down to a science. This one was so different. It was funny how we cried for change and then cried some more once we got it. My old one was certainly not waterproof, but this one claimed it was. I'd get used to this one. Still, that was one great week. By some miracle, I'd had no symptoms, and by accident I'd had no annoying calls. I couldn't have planned it better. *Maybe not getting so many calls made the headaches go away,* I thought. *Maybe not getting calls doesn't cure the headaches, but getting them certainly does contribute. If only it were that simple. Well, off home. I know Rachael wants me to stop for milk. We have probably used this week's allotment.*

Rachael called again. I said," Yes, milk. I got it. I'm psychic. I'll be there shortly."

I grabbed my coat and dashed for the door. Then I quickly ran my errands and scooted home. Dinner was ready and delicious as usual. I admit it was nice being a doctor: I got a decent allotment – better than the blue collars: more food, more petrol, more overall privileges. Still, the government was decent to everyone. No one went without. None of us had reason to complain; after all, we were all cogs in the same wheel. I just happened to fit into a nicer notch than some. *Well, I* am *a doctor,* I thought. That sounded arrogant, but I really did work hard to get where I was, and I didn't think recognizing that was arrogant.

I was about to enjoy a nice weekend, and there was nothing to do but relax. I had to take Jeremiah down for his own personal communication device. Six months before their tenth birthday, children were assigned a personal communicator. The epidemic didn't hit you until puberty or thereabout, however kids didn't enter puberty at the exact same age, so we started giving children the medicine just after the toddler years, to get their bodies adapted to it. It was a smaller dose than what adults took. Then just before children reached ten years of age, they were assigned their own communication device, in case something went wrong or there was a medical emergency as they entered the infected age. It made sense, and as a doctor, I completely agreed. It was sound, logical thinking.

Strange that Dad said Grandpa and his mates were always griping about the government interfering with their lives. I didn't get that at all. After all, the government helped us live better lives. They gave us work, educated us, and informed us about global issues and interests. Not to mention the quick response to the rapid spread of the epidemic and the development of a medicine to keep the symptoms to a minimum. Government was there every step of our lives to assist in anything and everything, like a government should.

I sounded like an advert for the state, but I supposed I was. All those years of greed and selfishness, the centuries of getting it wrong, and we finally had it right. We may still have a few problems, but it was a nearly perfect setup in my opinion. Government control was the safest and best life.

Saturday eventually came. Jeremiah and I headed to the communicator exchange for his assigned device. He chose a red one; it was cool, he said. To think that in two years, I'd be bringing Talia down here for hers. They grew up so fast. It was strange to know there was still no way to prevent them from getting this horrible disease. I wished there was. I saw so much disease and suffering as a doctor. At least when they got it, they got a cool device with all the latest technology. This device of Jeremiah's had all the best e-tools. It monitored his vital signs, had an instant global locator, and interfaced with his education terminal to ensure alerts for all assignments and reports due. I was not terribly sure that was a plus to a child, but as a parent I liked it. When I was a kid and we got sick, all we got were lots of needles taking stuff out and putting stuff in – and pills, pills, pills. It seemed like the dark ages sometimes, and yet at others times it didn't seem so long ago.

A nice quiet evening and a good night's rest was in order. I had a quiet evening, but not a good night's rest. My mind was racing with questions and curiosity. *Nine days of feeling fine. Nine days of no medicine. I'm not obsessed with solving the mystery. But still, why? Why me? Why nine days, and how? How did it happen?* The weekend came and went, as it usually did.

CHAPTER 12

Work was good on Monday, for once. The unusually happy Mrs Dumfries was no bother at all today – we even finished early for a change. "Want me to help you with the weekly reports?" Jacob said.

"Really? It's my night. You don't have to."

"Yeah," he replied. "And if we get a move on, we'll both be home early."

"Okay, let's do it. I suppose I owe you now," I said.

"Tell me what's on your mind, and we'll call it even."

"What do you mean?" I asked innocently. "I didn't think I had been too obvious about my situation."

"C'mon. Something's been on your mind for weeks. I may not be a psychic, but I *am* your brother. This is no different than that time in grammar school."

"What time?" I asked.

"You know," Jacob replied. "That time you were doolally tap for Haley Newbridge. You acted aloof, but it was all over your face for weeks."

"Wow! Haley Newbridge? The transfer student from Wales? I forgot all about her. Was I that obvious this week?"

"You haven't carved anything ridiculous into the tree out front, like you did back then. But yeah, I'd say it's been pretty plain to see that something is going on."

"You wouldn't believe it," I muttered.

"Try me."

I paused, took a deep breath, and then paused again. Like a bursting dam, I told him everything.

He didn't say anything at first. I could see his down-to-earth logic wheels turning, but it was clear that he was extremely intrigued. Then he started his deductive techniques. "Well, we know people in Kent are infected, so we can rule out anything to do with location. What about adrenaline? Did anything traumatic happen while you were there?"

"No," I replied. "I wrestled with my kids a bit in the pool, but otherwise nothing. The only thing out of the ordinary was my personal communicator taking a swim with me. Let me tell you, that was hardly traumatic – quite the opposite, in fact. It turned out to be downright peaceful."

"Hmm. So you really haven't had a pill in over a week?"

"Well, I hadn't had one. But like I said, after the nine days, it all came back. Now I'm back on the medicine."

"That is definitely a head scratcher. But it's late. I guess the mystery continues. I'll see you in the morning," he said.

"Good night, Jacob."

An early day for us was rare, so we wasted no time locking up and heading home. Halfway to the car, Jacob whirled around and yelled, "No matter the conclusion, it can't turn out worse than Haley Newbridge."

I had completely forgotten that, and for good reason. I had written her a love poem, tried to slip it to her in class, and got caught. Mr Lenahan read it in front of the whole class, and to make matters worse, I was punched in the head after class in the hallway by Stephen Hurst, who was apparently going steady with Haley (unbeknownst to me).

"Yes, let's hope," I yelled back.

It was nice that Jacob had such a razor-sharp memory of my adolescent humiliations. I got into my car and headed home. *Haley Newbridge*, I thought with a chuckle. *I wonder what happened to her. She probably looks like an old bus seat now. Ouch, what a horrid thing to say about someone. Well, all I know is she sure was pretty in those days.*

For the next few days, Jacob and I tossed around speculations, but we had nothing even remotely plausible.

Rachael called. "Hello?" I answered. "Yes, dear. Another allotment of milk. I'll get it." I hung up. "Boy, between work and home, this thing rings non-stop. Ever wish you could just chuck it?"

"What? Your communicator?" Jacob replied.

"No, not just the communicator. The whole thing – the communicator, the practice, the responsibilities, the constant complaints from patients, everything. Just chuck it."

"Of course," he replied. "I suspect everyone thinks about packing it in at least once in his life. It'll never happen, though," he said sternly.

"No, never happen," I said. "Well, except for my week of paradise."

"What week of paradise? Oh, right – your time off from the job, the calls, and the disease. Yeah, I'll bet that was …" Jacob paused. "No blooming way!"

"What? What is it?" I shouted.

"You didn't have the symptoms while you didn't have your communicator."

"What?"

"Perhaps it's your communicator."

"Are you insane? A phone cannot cause a disease, let alone an epidemic," I stated.

"You would think not, but it's the only thing that adds up. Try leaving your communicator at home for a week. Just don't bring it. Come on – turn it off and put it away for a week. Just try it."

"I can't do that!" I said. "Do you know how much I use this thing in a day, let alone a week? I can't be without it."

"What did you do the week it was off?" Jacob inquired.

"Well, I called the service from Rachael's phone and had all the calls forwarded to here or home."

"Right, just do that. Apart from the drive to and from work, you won't miss a thing. If I'm wrong, we've at least tested a theory."

"Okay, you are on," I replied. "But if you're wrong, we try the next experiment on *you*."

That night I turned off the communicator and put it in my nightstand. I then skipped the pill and turned in. Sure enough, right on schedule came the symptoms. I fumbled for my pills and lay there in the darkness in pain. *What a stupid idea,* I thought. My only solace was knowing that the next time, Jacob would be the guinea pig.

The next morning, Jacob was eagerly waiting. "Well? Tell me something," he said when I was barely out of my car.

I quickly replied, "Nothing! Your theory was extremely faulty."

"No," he said. "It has to be the right. It's your communication device. Are you sure it was off?"

"Yes, I'm very sure."

"Hmm, I'm thinking," Jacob said. We walked into the office.

The day went by fairly uneventful and was over before we knew it. "Well?" I said to him as we locked the door and headed to our cars.

"Well what?" he replied.

"Any new ideas?"

"Nope, not a clue."

We left and made our way to our houses for the evening.

The next morning was going to change everything. As I pulled in, Jacob was running towards my car before it parked. He practically pulled me through the window.

"What?" I said.

"I did it. I bleedin' did it!" he shouted.

"What did you do?"

"I found the glitch, and I fixed it."

"And what would the glitch be?" I inquired.

"These devices are smarter than we think. Even when they're off, they emit signals. I removed the battery and put the device into my safe. I skipped my pill and am feeling great."

"I can see that," I agreed.

"Tonight, you try it," he said.

Try it I did. Friday rolled around, and we saw the last patient out.

"Well?" Jacob asked.

"One week," I replied. "I did it all week, and it worked. You?"

"Yep, me too. No communicator, no pills, no symptoms."

"So we have the exact same results, except I also have no milk. It's to do with the lack of communicator. Are we to believe that these devices are responsible for an entire epidemic?" I asked.

"Well, I don't know for sure," Jacob replied. "But it's a starting point. We've got something to build on, so let's start sorting out this whole thing."

CHAPTER 13

The next day, we decided we would proceed slowly and carefully. We were two intelligent, educated, professional men, and we could not give in to the temptation to start playing detective. We simply took a scientific approach, just simple reasoning and deduction – none of this half-witted government conspiracy stuff, with wild accusations and crazy theories. We didn't approach it like there was some underlying deviousness at play here. We'd all known of men like that in the history of this great world – men who tried to dirty the good name of the state, who never saw the greater good, and never understood that we owed our loyalty to community and government. No, these conspirators were not men. They were filth, garbage, and traitors. Quite frankly, we were all glad to see them eradicated. Jacob and I were loyal to the state. We were thankful, we were true, and we were patriots.

A few weeks passed, and we went through dozens, maybe even hundreds of theories. Nothing made sense, and nothing fit. Problems were like jigsaw puzzles. Some pieces seemed to fit and belong there, but they didn't snap into place. You know that clean crisp snap that a puzzle piece has when it truly does belong? You feel it with your fingertips as you lay that piece down and sense the hard snap as it slots into place? You don't even have to look twice; you know it fits, it belongs. We hadn't felt that snap yet.

Another Friday came, and we ended the day as usual, but we

were frustrated and feeling desperate. Despite our best efforts, we gave in and started to play detective.

"What are the facts?" Jacob asked.

I replied, "Well, we are both without any sort of personal communication devices, we both have no symptoms, and …"

"And what?"

"Well, I feel more … well, um …"

"Clear," Jacob blurted.

"Yes, clear," I said. "Aggressive, driven, really in control."

"Me too. I mean, there is a feeling, a clarity, and a genuine desire to keep going, to push ahead no matter what the consequences. But what does it all mean? The world had mobile communication devices decades before the epidemic. The disease is only five years old. A few years ago, none of us had this ruddy thing."

I said, "Do we notify the authorities? Don't we have an obligation to report what's going on?"

"No!" Jacob said sternly. "What exactly would we tell them, anyway? We don't really know anything. We haven't made a single conclusion. We have nothing but a tiny experiment. We need more."

"More? How do we get more?" I said.

"Why don't we take the wives off it too?"

"Are you sure we want to start running experiments on our wives? I already tried once, and it didn't end well. The ruddy symptoms this disease brings with it are dreadful. I'm not sure I want to put them through that on a whim."

"I would agree completely – if it were a whim," Jacob replied. "But this is certainly no whim. Please, David, just give it a try."

"All right," I said. "I'll give it a try. But how do we pull it off? Do we tell them?"

"No, not just yet. Tell her your com device is giving you trouble, and you need to borrow hers."

"And the pills?"

"That one's tougher," he said. "Wait – we're doctors. We can replace their pills with something from around here, something that doesn't do anything. I'll whip something up. We can wait till the month rolls over and it's time for the new supply. Then we switch our placebo pills for the real ones and send a note saying they are replacing the pills with capsules for a month, to see if they are more effective. They aren't suspicious women and won't suspect anything."

"Brilliant!" I exclaimed. "That plan is a winner."

I realize that I stated at the beginning of this story that epidemic pills were the only ones not shipped to people's homes, and that they had to be picked up in person. However, there were a few exceptions, and one of them was a doctor's office. We were allowed to have our supplies shipped to the office because we were a designated emergency pickup facility. That meant that we stocked, though under lock and scan of course, with large supplies for emergencies such as a chemist shop fire or late shipments. Jacob and I had our personal prescriptions forwarded to our homes. It was a bit on the edge of the rules, but it was not technically breaking any.

The month ended, and our renewal shipments came in the post like clockwork. I called Rachael and asked her to lunch, as Jacob and I had planned. She said sure and headed to the clinic. I headed home. The post had run, and I quickly opened Rachael's package and replaced her pills with the fake ones. Then I slipped in the phony note, resealed the package, and put it back into the box. I rushed back to the office. I had been very tight with driving lately, so my fuel cell allotment shouldn't be affected. I arrived with a story about needing to run a quick errand, and Rachael and I headed to eat. We returned, and I quickly got rid of Rachael without making it look like it. Jacob returned and told me that he had done the same.

The day wound down, and we headed home. The next morning, we both arrived at work, disabled com devices in hand. We put them into the medicine vault and waited for the results. Friday rolled around, and the results were as suspected: the wives had had no symptoms – absolutely none at all. We had come to a very definite conclusion: personal communication devices caused the epidemic.

But instead of fewer questions this conclusion raised many more.

I couldn't bear thinking about them at present, with the exception of the obvious ones. How did we tell the world? *Should* we tell the world? Would anyone believe us? Would everyone on earth be willing to go without mobile communication devices? And why should they? After all, the pill kept all symptoms in check. Why hadn't we as a society come up with a communication device that didn't cause an epidemic by now? And how exactly did it cause the epidemic, anyway? It didn't add up.

There was one extra side effect. Jacob and I discovered that while on the pill, we were much more docile, more easygoing and agreeable. We were less opinionated, less aggressive, less assertive, less … Well, to be honest, we were less real.

CHAPTER 14

The next morning, we opened up the office as usual and began our daily routine, but with an odd feeling floating around in the air. I didn't exactly know whether the feeling could be pinned down to a simple one, like happiness, anger, or grief. Those were all very exact feelings. This feeling was one that I knew was there but couldn't quite assign a title to, except to say it was strange. After all, we knew a secret no one else knew. Well, somebody else knew it. Somebody else *had* to know it. Maybe we were the only people at the bottom who knew it, but somebody way up at the top had to know. After all, they'd created it, hadn't they?

We worked our normal day and didn't say much about it until the last patient had gone home. Jacob said, "Well, what do we do now? Do we investigate further on our own? Do we tell the authorities? Or do we just forget about it?"

"We forget about it," I said. "What is the big deal? I mean, who is really getting hurt here? For now, it appears this epidemic is not as they say it is. They must have their reasons, I mean, it's not like the world's government needs to consult the two of us whenever a problem arises. Lots of big problems arise and are dealt with every day, without us being privy to any of them. I bet at the very worst, it's a plan to keep the pharmaceutical companies selling drugs to everyone on the planet – a money-making scheme. It's happened before. I'll bet the rising cost of research has pushed these companies to do this in order to create necessary income for much-needed testing and development of new drugs. This tactic is easier than coming right out and saying they need more money, because people would complain. They always do. Besides, it's much bigger than us. I say no harm, no foul. There's nothing wrong with the world – well, nothing too terribly wrong with it. Why mess with it?"

"Nothing wrong with the world?" Jacob said loudly. "Every human being above the age of three has to take a pill every single day for symptoms that come from the use of a personal communication device. It's a device, might I remind you, that they say we must have because of the disease – which we wouldn't have if we didn't have personal communication devices! It's insane, and there's no way you can expect me to believe that 'more money for research' mumbly jumbly you just prattled off. I don't even believe that *you* believe that."

"No, I suppose I don't, not truly," I responded. "But all we have is a theory. We're not even qualified experts in this area. This isn't life shattering. Let's not go poking around; we've done enough already."

"Why doesn't this matter to you?" Jacob scolded.

"I don't know. Why does it matter to you?" I replied quickly.

"Because for one, it costs me over 150 pounds a month to buy the pills for me, my wife, and my son. That has come out of my pay for years, and for what? For pills that we should not need at all!"

"Okay," I said. "You tell me, then. What do we do? Where do we even start?"

"Well, for one thing, we start by figuring out how mobile communication devices have caused the human body to be in need of constant medicine, and how getting rid of those devices stops the symptoms immediately."

"How do we do that? So we go down to the mobile communication store? You think the guy behind the counter is going to tell us?"

Jacob rubbed his temples. "Okay, I see your point."

"This is disturbing, but don't you feel that everybody who's involved in this is so far up the ladder that they're beyond our reach?

No one is going to talk to us. They aren't going to give us access to anything relating to this. We're nobodies."

Jacob looked annoyed, but I could see he agreed. We simply didn't have any pull. "There's got to be someone we can talk to about this," he said. "There has to be somebody. I mean, we've been doctors for years. We went to university and interned. We know a lot of people."

"What about that doctor in Wales?" I asked. "The one who invented empathetic medicine. You know, the guy who invented these machines we use every day. He might know something about it. Well, not so much about the epidemic, but about how it's able to be done. I mean, he invented the transference of pain through electronic devices. I understand those symptoms are artificial, and the ones caused by these com devices are real, but it is the same concept as the way we use the machines we have here in the office, only on a smaller scale in the com device. At the very least, he may be able to tell us about how an electronic device is causing pain. I mean, we don't develop tumours or other physical things that can be removed through surgery. But the prolonged use of these things obviously causes pain that these pills seem to alleviate, even if we still don't know why."

"Or who exactly *they* are," Jacob replied. "Hang on a tick – I have an idea. Get onto the interweb terminal and do a gadget search. Pull up a map of the areas on the earth the epidemic affected for a sec. I want to have a look at something."

"It affected everyone," I said.

"No, no. It most certainly did not. There were some far-reaching places where people didn't go – some places in Australia and Africa. The disease didn't spread there. We have a theory that the use of personal communication devices causes the problem, yet we all think the disease is contagious, and so therefore access is limited to areas of the planet that are hard to reach. But if it actually isn't contagious, then why restrict access to anywhere? I mean, it's not necessary, is it?"

"All right," I said. "I've got the map of the infected area, but it won't help. I mean, look at it. The earth is almost completely covered."

"Yes, almost. But there are a few small places. far-reaching in some areas: Africa, New Zealand, New Guinea, Australia. Places out of the way where nobody ever goes. The people in those villages did not get affected by the disease. You see? You have to zoom in to notice them, but they're there."

I said, "Great, but how does that help us?"

"It's just a theory, but pull up a map from the mobile communication company that shows the areas they do not service."

"Got it."

"Now overlap it onto the epidemic map."

As I overlaid the maps, our jaws dropped. They were identical! Far-reaching places on the earth that had no communication service had no epidemic. Our theory was now fact. For some reason, somebody had started an epidemic by transmitting symptoms through our personal communication devices into our bodies. But how did they get into our bodies, and how could a phone make us feel sick or give us a headache? And why?"

"One of us has to go see this scientist who invented pain transference," Jacob said.

"Well, we can't both go. We have patients; one of us is going to have to stay here and cover," I said. "I just had my holiday, so it will look suspicious if I go again. You're due for a holiday, so you go."

"Okay," Jacob said. "Now I just have to convince my wife that we need a holiday in the north of Wales."

"Good luck with that."

This was starting to feel like one of those old spy movies they used to make before they were banned. Wouldn't that be cool, sneaking around with gun in hand, pretending to be businessmen and dignitaries? I was not sure I could use a gun; they were banned for good reason. The government taught us early on that only trained government representatives should have guns. Common citizens should never own or use guns, and crime now was practically non-existent because of that education. Still, the idea of being a secret agent appealed to most people.

Jacob made the necessary arrangements and convinced his wife that Wales was the ideal spot in which to properly enjoy a holiday. A few days went by, and then Jacob called. It was difficult for us to get in touch when neither of us had a mobile com device. He called me from the bed and breakfast in Llangollen.

"What's the story?" I asked.

"He's not here anymore," Jacob replied quickly. "Apparently, about six years ago he was offered a big job working for the government."

"Let me guess: London."

"No, the headquarters for this one is in Edinburgh. It's some kind of research and development program for the military. I'm not sure exactly what it is about. Nobody here knows very much. They did say that he left rather abruptly. Well, it really is beautiful here in Wales. I hate to cut a holiday short, but I'll make up some excuse and will head to Edinburgh first thing in the morning."

I said, "Scotland? Really? You're going to drop everything in Wales and head to Scotland tomorrow? I mean, how are you even going to explain that?"

"I'll think of something," Jacob said confidently.

"This really means a lot to you," I noted. "I don't understand that. It doesn't affect our lives in any way – not enough to go poking a hornets' nest. Why keep pursuing it?"

"Truth!" Jacob said sternly. "Don't you think it's important that we find out the truth? It doesn't matter whether it affects us or makes our lives better or worse. It matters whether we have been lied to. This is absolutely not about pills and headaches anymore. It's about truth, and I'm going to find out. David, don't you see? If they lie about this, what else do they lie about? Everything? We find out the truth no matter how long, and no matter the cost."

I was speechless. Was this my brother? Where was all this rage and passion coming from? He scared me with his speech, but he was right. I simply wasn't as enthused as he was about the truth.

"So the government had to hide a few things. So what?" I said. "We live pretty good – no, very good lives. Do we really need to botch that up? I don't see the need to mess with it."

The immediate silence was deafening. It shouted of the rift between us. We were in this together, but it was clear that we weren't together on principal. I didn't like that, but I couldn't see justifying risking the amount we had to lose.

CHAPTER 15

Thursday night rolled around. Jacob called me sounding very excited.

"I need you to get up here," he said. "I've made us an appointment for tomorrow morning with Dr McTarvish. Here's the plan. When you arrive, Gabriellah and Michael can take my car for the day. I'll ride with you to the meeting."

"Wait a minute," I said. "What about tomorrow's patients? We have a tendency to see our patients each day. It's called a job. You know – responsibility and all that petty hogwash."

"David, sarcasm is not your bailiwick," Jacob retorted. "You'll think of something. You're very clever when you choose to be. Bye." He quickly hung up.

Bloomin' easy for him. I've got a few hours to find someone to cover my patients tomorrow. This just keeps getting better, I thought.

Morning came, and I headed out early. The whole way up, I kept thinking of how utterly useless it was to mess with a system of life and government that worked well. At first it seemed okay to do a little prying because of the irresistible curiosity and the excitement of a mystery. I led a fairly mundane life, so when something adventurous came along, it was hard to resist. But now some time has passed, and the weight of this thing became a reality. I couldn't stop thinking about needlessly getting into trouble.

I arrived at the hotel and picked up Jacob. He said good-bye to Gabriellah and Michael and then got into the car. We didn't speak much on the way. It wasn't awkward; we both felt that because we were in disagreement about the importance of this situation, any discussion could lead to a fight. I supposed it was a polite silence.

We arrived at the facility and informed them of our meeting with Doctor McTarvish. They took us into the guard gate building, scanned us, and double-checked our physical IDs. Then they asked us for our automobile interface code. This was the code that allowed our automobile's central onboard terminal to "talk" to their central command terminal. Basically, it unlocked the car to allow new instructions from a terminal other than the government global position and guidance system – the one who drove the car.

We finished up and returned to the car. Once we turned it on, the onboard information screen displayed the new information from the guard gate. It was a guided route to Doctor McTarvish's office without the option to override. Our car would only drive to the doctor's research lab and nowhere else, until we exited the facility. This was standard procedure on a tightly run, high-security base such as this.

It was a real hybrid of a facility: part research and development lab, and part military installation. But still, why were there so many men with guns patrolling? Most bases had armed security guards walking around, but this was two, maybe three times the usual. The place was crawling with armed personnel everywhere we looked.

We arrived at the office. We walked through a huge steel door, which closed behind us, locking us between it and another huge steel door. A voice came over the speaker. "Hold still for scanning, gentlemen." A beam swept across the room from front to back, from side to side, and then from floor to ceiling.

"Ouch!" Jacob shouted. "Did you feel that? He looked panicked.

"No, I didn't feel anything. Are you okay?" I asked. "Did it hurt? What did it feel like?"

"Nothing," Jacob replied. "I just wanted to see the look on your face. I didn't feel a thing!" He chuckled.

"You know," I said matter-of-factly, "I think I liked you better on the pill. Try to keep your new-found sense of humour to yourself in this meeting, if you could."

The steel door in front of us rumbled open, and the voice instructed us to step through.

"Good morning, Doctors," McTarvish said. "I bet you are here to discuss my machine."

"We are," I replied. I was surprised at how could he know why we were there.

"Well, there really is nothing to say that the online tutorials and classes don't already tell you. If you two are practicing physicians, then I can assume you have both been extensively trained on it."

"Of course," said Jacob. "We are both up to current compliance on the machine and its workings. But we've run into something else in our work and were wondering whether your machine was only capable of transference of feelings from one person to another."

"Oh, no," said Dr McTarvish. "My machine is extremely complex. The earlier models were bigger and, for lack of a better word, clunky. They were very limited on what they could do. But this latest model is amazing. In fact, that's why I am here. You see, in the field an empathic symptom machine is perfect for transferring symptoms from patient to doctor in order to seek out an exact disease or ailment for the fastest medical treatment or cure. From time to time, it has detected early symptoms to enable the prevention of disease.

"But we found that in the universities, we had to constantly find people with diseases in order to show students what a disease felt like. You can't transfer the symptoms of a disease if you don't have someone with that disease, now, can you? I'm telling you, it's not easy to find every kind of disease known to man – and locally, at that. Then that same person with the disease has to be willing to come to our university hospitals to be hooked to my machine so that medical students can learn which disease is which. As you might suspect, that is a monstrous task. Therefore the government hired me and moved me here to create a program that assigns algorithms to each micro symptom. These millions, and in some cases even billions, of micro symptoms are combined to mimic whatever disease or ailment we assign to it."

Jacob interrupted. "So basically, your new database allows you to hook a patient up, record his feelings, and play them back through the machine for each student long after the patient is gone."

"Well put, Doctor," McTarvish replied. "However, as I said earlier, it is by no means that simple. Do you understand what it takes to digitally record billions of microns of pain and then categorize them, log them, sort them, and so on? Do you know we have almost three-quarters of the world's diseases recorded?"

"That's amazing," I said.

"You'd think that, wouldn't you? But these first recordings, if you want to call them that, did not turn out right."

"What do you mean?" I asked.

"When transferred to the physician for diagnoses, the symptoms felt ..." He paused.

"Felt what?"

"Fake," he finally replied.

"Fake?" Jacob repeated. "What do you mean, fake?"

"I really do hate using these crude words; they don't do the situation justice. But yes, for the sake of getting my point across, they were fake – not real. When put into the doctor or student, they lacked reality."

"I don't understand," I said.

"Well, we don't either, do we? I mean, we're working with feelings here. It's all new territory. I invented a machine to transfer the feelings of a real patient into a real human doctor in real time, at the point of contact, that is totally different than storing feelings for – again, crude terminology – replay later. It's all new, uncharted waters. We are flying blind. It's not only never been done, but it's never been thought of."

"Till now," I said.

"Till now," the doctor agreed. "Gentlemen, I can't explain

exactly how the feelings felt fake; they just did. Those of us hooked to the machines knew the feelings were artificial. We all have feelings from conception and use them every day. Believe me, you know a false one when it comes along."

Jacob said, "When your new database machine is finished, could you send any symptom to anyone, anywhere?"

"Oh, no," said Dr McTarvish. "You have to be hooked to the machine to have the empathic signals sent to you.

"You couldn't do it wirelessly?" Jacob asked.

"That's correct. Feelings transference is a massive endeavour. It simply cannot be done wirelessly. I know most of our equipment is wireless, but what you are getting at is simply impossible. Doctors, I'm starting to feel as if you have something specific you are here for."

Jacob paused. "Well, let me tell you what happened to my brother."

After hearing my story about being on vacation, the doctor look disturbed for a second and then simply said, "Coincidence. Fluke. It was a one-time random event. It happens, you know. Your body has had the medicine put into it for so long that it builds up a stored amount – an extra few doses, if you like – either in the pancreas or the bloodstream. But as you know, not too much. When you stopped taking medicine, this excess in the body relieved you of your symptoms for a short time. We haven't quite figured out everything in medicine yet. But of course you're both doctors; I suspect you knew that already."

"It could have been a situation as you just described," Jacob replied. "The thing is, though, we tried it a few weeks later on with me. Same results."

Dr McTarvish replied, "I think you're reading too much into this. Truly, Doctors, all we have here is a tempest in a teapot. I really do have a busy day. It all sounds quite interesting, but not earth-shattering. If you will excuse me." With that, he left quickly.

As he was exiting the room, Jacob yelled, "Well, back to the Knights Inn for us, then. Thank you, Doctor."

Jacob and I just stood there staring at each other. "May I ask you something?" Jacob said.

"Sure," I replied.

"Did you believe the stored medicine explanation? Tell the truth."

"Believe it? I'm amazed that he even proposed it, especially to us."

"Yeah. And how about that exit? Talk about abrupt."

I replied, "But even so, I keep feeling that we're getting nowhere."

"Getting nowhere? Jacob repeated. "Are you kidding? He's hiding something. It was obvious! We've got a lot more than nowhere." He smirked.

"Are you listening to yourself? This is crazy. Maybe he is hiding something, but you heard what he said about his research. What we are proposing isn't possible, and by his own admittance. The next step in the evolution of empathic medicine is still only theory. Did you hear all the trouble he's having? I say enough is enough. Let's go home."

"You are right," Jacob said, which surprised me. "No fuss, no problem. But let's stay at the hotel one more night. I like the Knights Inn, and I *am* on holiday." We left through the same painstaking process by which we entered the base, and we got back to the room and sat for a minute.

"Dinner?" I suggested.

"Absolutely! There's a pub downstairs, and I hear it's fantastic."

We ate and headed back to the room. As we arrived at the door, we saw Dr McTarvish waiting.

"Hello, Doctor," Jacob said cockily, as if he was expecting him.

"I was hoping there weren't too many Knights Inns in Edinburgh," McTarvish said.

CHAPTER 16

As we sat in the room, the doctor apologised for his sudden departure during our meeting. He explained that there were cameras all over the building, and he wasn't comfortable talking there. "After all," he explained, "It is a maximum security facility."

Jacob must have known this. Why else would he specifically give the hotel name so loudly as we were leaving? He knew McTarvish was going to need it to find us. I'd thought he had lost his mind, but it seemed Jacob was quite cunning. Still, I'd let the jury deliberate a bit longer on his sanity.

"So why come to our hotel?" I asked. "I mean, what couldn't be said at your facility? Are you hiding something?"

"Well, yes and no," he replied cryptically. "You see, after my invention eight years ago, the medical business was healing at an amazing rate. It was a genuinely good thing, but the pharmaceutical companies took a massive hit. No trial-and-error pill buying anymore. The united global authority decided a boost was needed. They asked me to create symptoms that could be carried through a mobile device, but they wanted every symptom known to man. In other words, an artificial back spasm for you, but a massive headache for your brother; a sore shoulder for Mr Jones, and a tender ankle for Mrs Smith."

"I get it!" yelled Jacob. "We all continue our lives healthier because of your machine, but with a smattering of artificial aches and pains of millions of different varieties, which seem quite normal to most people, especially those of advanced age. Therefore we continue buying medicine at the usual rate, spending trillions a year for relief from ailments."

"Ailments we don't really have!" I burst out.

McTarvish said, "That's right. The ailments would be quite artificial."

"But?" I prompted.

"But you don't all have different symptoms. You all have the same symptoms. Is that your question, Doctor?" McTarvish said. "As I explained earlier, we haven't been able to properly log and reproduce all sicknesses yet, or transfer them wirelessly. Years ago in my earlier research, I found a way to transfer only a handful of ailments, and it was quite an undertaking to get these to transfer wirelessly. Unfortunately, I haven't been able to get any further. All we had was a small number of symptoms for an entire world. Well, governments aren't big on waiting, so they said, 'Give those few symptoms to everyone.' Then boom – an epidemic was started, at least in the civilized world. Any place so remote that mobile technology didn't reach was remote enough to easily be passable for a disease-free zone, because few people ever came and went from those areas."

"So you hook us all on drugs!" I shouted. "You're a doctor, remember. Do no harm."

"Gentlemen, you can't have an 'all the drug companies are broke' tax," he replied. "A lot of economies would crash overnight if the pharmaceutical companies went under. You cannot collapse a world economy overnight. It would be worse than a nuclear war. In war, people die. You don't have to feed dead people. But to have a financial disaster of this magnitude is far worse because no one dies. There are ruined financial markets, but no one is dead. Millions of people would be out of jobs and money, and they still need to eat, have shelter, and be clothed. This was the best solution. It's not a perfect world, after all.

"The plan was a ten-year concept. We would create better drugs each year and slowly wean everyone off the drug. That allowed drug companies a decade to adjust and downsize accordingly. It wasn't flawless, but it was necessary."

Jacob growled, "Meanwhile, I'm doling out 150 pounds a month for nothing!"

I interrupted. "It's been five years, so it's half over? I mean the downsizing and all that? We ride it out for just five more years, and it's all over?"

"Not exactly," McTarvish replied. "You see, with the unrest within the Asian federation, and the trouble being stirred up in the Middle East around Soviet Palestine, global money is tight. It may be another few years over the ten. The council hasn't decided yet. There are a lot of factors at play here. However, they have decided that if you two are willing to sign a document of secrecy, you will not have to pay for your medicine ever again, and you will be reimbursed all the money you have spent to date."

"Deal!" I yelled.

"Hey!" Jacob said. "A document of secrecy?"

"Yes," McTarvish replied. "Gentleman you have stumbled upon something that is not public knowledge, and neither do we wish it to be. We keep our research facilities secure for a reason. They quite rightly expect you to sign a document saying that you will abide by the same code of secrecy as anyone associated with the program. I think that is not asking too much."

"Not so blooming fast," Jacob said. "That's it? That's all? We just found out the biggest plague in the history of the world is a fake, and we're supposed to sign an agreement and go home, never mentioning it again?"

McTarvish said, "I'm just a doctor at a research facility. I have no power to wheel and deal. I was told to make this offer, and I suggest you take it. It's a good offer."

"I suppose we have no choice," Jacob said.

"Funny thing," McTarvish said. "Your accident happened just in time. In a few years, it would have been impossible."

"What do you mean?" I asked.

"Well, the United Global Authority decided that by the end of next year, the PIC would be mandatory, and paper money would be done away with."

"What's a PIC?" I asked.

"It's that little chip in your hand," Jacob said. "Personal information chip. Didn't you read the pamphlet they gave you when you got it?"

"No, I don't need to because I knew you would, and then you'd explain it to me condescendingly," I shot back.

Dr McTarvish continued. "The next-generation chip is so powerful that we no longer need a mobile device. We can send the symptoms right to the person. So you see, in a year or two, diving into a pool with your phone would not have stopped the symptoms, and you'd be none the wiser. Mandatory implantation is no big deal. Half the population already has the old chip."

"And that's it? You're doing away with all paper money?" I asked.

"Not just paper money," the doctor explained. "All the different currencies. They are obsolete in a unified digital economy. They have decided to settle on one global currency."

"And what currency would that be?" I enquired. "The dollar? The yen?"

"No," McTarvish said. "They have decided to use an old form of money used primarily in Germany, before the European superstate and the euro. They called it the deutsche mark back then. Now it will simply be called the global mark. All countries will be on the same currency, and a few years later we'll 'cure' the disease. It's a very clever way to save the world economy and avoid a global panic."

"And all you had to do was sell your soul," Jacob snarled.

"We are doctors," McTarvish quickly replied. "We both know there's no such thing as a soul. I'm helping bring unity to the world while keeping major business from collapsing. It's a perfectly respectable living. Sign the papers and go back to your practices,

Doctors. You've stumbled onto something and were understandably curious, but now it's been explained to you. This is the end of the road."

We both signed the papers, and McTarvish left.

CHAPTER 17

As we drove back home the next morning, I could clearly see that Jacob was not happy. "Come on," I said. "We are no longer paying for the pills, and we are getting reimbursed for all the years of having to buy them. We're heading back to lives we were extremely happy with."

"No, David!" he yelled. "We weren't extremely happy. We were mildly content. We were not extremely anything. You may think the world is near perfect and getting more so every day, but I don't. One huge thing was missing from that meeting. McTarvish never explained why the pills alter our moods. Why do they make us so docile? He could have explained it as a side effect or some other hokey nonsense that Joe off the street would buy into. But we are doctors, and we know better. So instead of a ridiculous lie, he said nothing. Although everything else he said made sense, it's the principle that the world was put on drugs against its will and without its knowledge. It's wrong, David."

"I know, Jacob," I replied. "I do feel the same way. But what can we do? We're nobodies."

"I know," he said, sounding very defeated. "But explain this to me. He offered us a deal from the government."

"And?"

"And he did it in our hotel room under the veil of secrecy. If that was a government proposal, and they okayed it, he could have done it back at the research facility, at the base. There'd be no need to sneak over to our room. But then, you picked up on that too."

"Yes," I replied timidly. "I picked up on that too."

"I knew you did. I'm not that much smarter than you. Better looking? Sure. But not smarter."

"I simply didn't know what to make of it," I replied.

"Neither did I," Jacob confessed.

I paused. "Well, it's over now. We scanned our IDs onto that secrecy form. And anyway, who told you that you were better looking than me? Your girlfriend in primary school? Shelia Watkins – the one with the bad eyes?"

"Hey!" Jacob said. "She had an astigmatism, but she knew a good thing when she saw one. Plus, she let me into her tree house. May I ask you a question?"

"Sure."

"Why did you sign that document of secrecy?"

"Funny – I was going to ask you the exact same question. To be blatantly honest, it was fear. I think the surrealness of the situation came into focus. Each time we made a discovery, this thing got bigger, and I felt so much smaller. In the end, I was terrified, so I signed. And you?"

"The same," he replied. "There was something about the way he said 'I suggestion you take the offer' that came across like we didn't want to know what would happen if we didn't."

We finally arrived home and agreed to keep our wives out of the whole incident. "I'll see you tonight," I said as I got into my car.

"Tonight?" he asked.

"Mum and Dad are coming over for dinner."

"Oh, right," he said. "Yes, tonight. Cheers."

I drove home, freshened up, and rested a bit on the bed. As I lay there staring at the ceiling, my mind was focused on only one thing. Well, two things. First of all, the ceiling could use a fresh coat. Second, I thought about McTarvish. Why did my gut keep telling me that he wasn't wrapping up an incident for the government? I really felt as if he was baiting a hook. I knew the actions of that day said otherwise, but there was something in his inflections, in his voice, and in his face that said, "Keep digging." My mind was so heavy with thoughts that I slowly faded to sleep.

I was awakened by a tap on my shoulder. It was Talia. "Mum says Grandma and Grandpa will be here in an hour," she said.

"Thanks, love," I said, still in a fog. "Wait, come back and sit with your dad a bit." Talia was such an easygoing kid. She was very close to me and was an extraordinarily wise nine-year-old. She lay on the bed next to me and rested her head on my shoulder.

"Baby," I said, "what would you do if something was bothering you? If you ... uh, well, if you knew something that maybe you should tell people?"

"Is it for the greater good of the world?" she asked

"What?"

"Is it for the greater good? Does it follow the guidelines of the things that help us?"

"Where did you learn to talk like this?" I asked.

"At school," she replied. "It's in my handbook: *Ethics of Global Unity.*"

"Oh, yes. I remember I had that book in school."

It had just been released when I was coming up. Before the new curriculum came out, people were incredibly self-motivated, trying to succeed instead of promoting the collective. The new standard of learning erased that mindset and taught people to think of the community and government first. She was right: it was for the greater good that I get on with my life and forget all this nonsense.

"Thank you, dear. That helped."

"I didn't really say anything, Dad."

"Oh, you said enough, love. Now, go tell your mum I'll be right down."

I pulled myself together and headed downstairs to greet everyone. Jacob was right on time with Gabriellah and Michael; Mum and Dad were seconds behind them. We had a nice meal, and the conversation was nice. However, I could still see Jacob was uneasy. We finished and went into the reception room for tea.

"So, boys, any new breakthroughs in modern medicine this week?" Dad said.

I almost burst out laughing, and not because it was funny. It was more a defence mechanism triggered just before an emotional breakdown. Jacob looked like a pressure cooker about to explode. Clearly we were handling this differently.

I dismissed his question. "Dad, how are your knees?"

"Oh, I suppose they aren't too bad," he replied.

Then Jacob spoke up. "Dad, what was life like when you were a kid? Was it like it is now?"

"Oh, no," Dad said. "But it was progressing this way. We weren't quite the smooth-running society we've seem to become in your lifetime. There were still quite a few rough edges and dodgy bits in society when I was growing up. You know, if you really want to know what life was like in a different world, you need to talk to my dad."

"Grandpa? Really?" I said. Our grandpa was a bit of a strange one. He believed in outdated superstitions and nonsense, fairies and magic dust, and all the fantasy business. He had embraced an archaic form of extremism late in life, called Christianity. It was based on a God above but was centred primarily around another God on earth who was related to the God in the sky. Not only was it bad for society, but apparently it was very bad for someone of Hebrew descent to be one. I didn't know much about it. Religion was obsolete and so divisive that the government had to shut it down. It wasn't hard because most people didn't care. It was a load of old nonsense and superstitions, so it was not too difficult to get rid of for a logically thinking and fact-driven society.

"Let's go tomorrow after work," Jacob said.

"All right, you two!" Rachael blasted. "What's going on? You have both been acting very strangely."

"I agree," Gabriellah chimed in.

"Tell them," I said.

"No," Jacob replied.

"Tell us! Tell us, tell us!" the ladies harmonized, almost as if it was rehearsed.

"We cannot," Jacob said sternly. "It's to do with work, and we yet aren't cleared to talk about it publicly."

Wow, good one, I thought to myself. I added, "When it's time, you girls will absolutely be the first to know. You know that."

"Fine," Rachael said. "I know two guys who aren't getting custard on their jam roly-poly."

I blurted out, "For custard, I'll confess anything! Even the obsession of an eight-year-old boy with a strange, wall-eyed girl simply because she had a tree house."

"She had an astigmatism!" Jacob yelled.

Gabriellah looked curious and slightly annoyed. I may have gotten Jacob into trouble, but at least they weren't thinking about our secret anymore.

CHAPTER 18

Monday was a regular workday: lots of patients – and grumpy ones too. I'd picked up a new one, and the man was none too pleasant. *Jacob gets all the nice ones, and the buggers all gravitate to me. I add days to their lives, and they take years off mine. Seems like a fair trade.*

I made it through. I was thoroughly amazed at how some patients couldn't be dragged in, even when dying, and others showed up for every ache or hangnail. As we wrapped up the day, I felt less and less like seeing the old man as usual. In direct opposition to how I felt, it would appear Jacob couldn't wait. *I may have to kill him.* I smirked embarrassingly because I was the only one to find that amusing, especially because I didn't say it out loud.

"Let's go find out about life before perfection," Jacob quipped.

We rang our wives to remind them of our heartfelt pangs of nostalgia; we just had to go see dear old Grandpa. The sad thing was it should have been the truth. I didn't ever spend any time with Grandpa, or even think about him that much. I consoled myself with the fact that I was a busy doctor with a full life and many responsibilities.

We headed to the pensioners' facility, a huge, dark grey, brick building that from some angles could be mistaken for a penitentiary or asylum. Maybe in the back of people's minds was the thought that we were all heading there, and so we wished to spend as little time as possible there in the meantime. Maybe that was why the people here had so few visitors. Or maybe the truth was we simply shipped off our elderly to these places and forgot about them. Maybe that was the truth we wished to avoid.

We stopped at the gate, scanned in, and headed to his room. We knocked, and Grandpa opened the door. "Well, my little guys. How wonderful to see you. Come in, come in. Your father told me you were coming," he said. "You had a lot of questions about the past. If that's true, you must want to know about how it was when the dinosaurs roamed the earth. We got our food and our wives the same way: we clubbed them over their heads and dragged them back to the caves!"

"Oh, come now, Grandpa. You're not that old," I said.

"In fact, you look great," Jacob added.

Grandpa shook his head, amused. "All right, I have no money to lend, so cut that out right now. I look like a tired old man."

I said, "No, you really do look good. And not just your health. I mean, it's just good to see you. We certainly aren't here for money. We just want to know about the old days. Well, not old. You know, about life when you were a child."

"Tell you what, boys. I'm going to set some conditions," he said mysteriously.

"Anything, Grandpa," we gladly agreed.

"All right, then. I'll tell you a few things today, but from now on, you will be told one thing on each visit, and you have to bring your families."

"Uh, why exactly is that, Grandpa?" I said.

"Because I said so, and I'm your grandpa. So do you agree or not?" We agreed. He made us both a nice cup of Earl Grey and told us about his birth and early years, as well as a little about his parents. They were small things, nothing too detailed, but they were interesting.

Then he said very sternly, "It's going to be very different from now on, so be ready and pay attention." Jacob and I agreed, puzzled though we were at that cryptic statement. Grandpa really was a nice bloke.

CHAPTER 19

The next day after work, we headed to get our kids and bring them with us to see Grandpa. We arrived and sat down.

Grandpa looked at all of us and said, "When Benjamin, your dad, was coming up, he must have eaten a million pounds of food, but I only fed him three times a day. Even if he was capable of holding a million pounds of food in one meal, I still would have fed him three meals a day. This was for two reasons. Number one, mealtime itself should be enjoyable. Number two, he needed time to digest the food one meal at a time. So you see, I'm going to tell you some things, but only what I feel you can take in one sitting. Then I'll give you time to digest it. Do you understand?"

We nodded in agreement. Over the next few weeks, Grandpa told us an array of stories about this land and others. He talked about how he used to mow people's lawns for money, and how at the end of movies, they would play the national anthem, and people would stand a sing along. He talked of a time when Britain and other countries were independent, chose their allies based on common goals, and freely elected their leaders. He told us about street vendors who would flood the high street on weekends, and about bullies in school who toughened up kids and taught them that life was going to give them some lumps, so they'd better be able to take them. He discussed jumping off a roof with an umbrella because he saw it in a movie, even though it never turned out the way it did in the movie. He reminisced about the time before insurance companies and governing bodies regulated everything we did, even children's play. They made forts of refrigerator boxes and tyre swings, before green mandates ordered immediate recycling. He talked about a world so imperfect that it was a paradise. He listed obtuse people who would be banned in today's world – names like Churchill, Reagan, Lincoln, Wellington, and Thatcher. He talked about them in a way that was far different than how they were described in our history books. They were real, gritty, imperfect, flawed people with integrity and guts. They despised tyranny in any form.

After weeks of history lessons, he said, "Tomorrow, we start on you." He pointed at each of us in the room. It was intimidating, but I couldn't wait.

CHAPTER 20

I lay in bed that night, thinking about it all. This was what Grandpa meant about digesting it all. I was certainly doing that, and it was all I could do to concentrate on my work each day. His life and perspective was so different than anything we had ever known or been taught.

The next night was a bit different. This time we had props, and he told me to bring three helium-filled balloons and two weights. The next day, we showed up, and Grandpa looked very stern. "Have a seat," he said. He then asked Michael and Jeremiah to join him. He gave each a balloon and each a weight. He told Jeremiah to drop the weight and release the balloon. The weight fell to the floor as the balloon drifted towards the ceiling. It seemed a pointless exercise. He then asked Michael to hold the weight above his head and hold the balloon to the ground. *This is strange,* I thought.

He looked us sternly in the face and said something that I will never forget. "Truth and lies are forever tethered, boys. But truth is, by its very nature, buoyant and floats without help, without assistance, without need of an external agent. It simply floats to the surface where it belongs. A lie is naturally heavy and will always sink without help. So when you release truth, it soars high for all to see. If you release a lie, it automatically sinks to the bottom. The opposite is also true." He gestured towards Michael, who was looking very uncomfortable at this point. "To tell a lie is to not only hold high this massive weight. You must continually hold down this truth that is constantly pushing upwards to be set free." Just then, Michael let out an enormous sigh, and as the balloon went up, that weight came down. The point was permanently nailed to my heart.

He elaborated. "When you say something that isn't true, you have to prop it up, and then you have to hold it up forever. That is extremely exhausting. At the same time, there will always be the truth out there, always pushing upwards to soar free. You're going to have to continually hold that thing down, out of sight. As Michael demonstrated a few seconds earlier, no one can keep a lie up and the truth down forever. No one can!"

Why had we waited until now to talk to this amazing man, this wealth of history and how life should be? Why didn't any of this get into our father – or if it did, why didn't he teach us? I didn't know whether the rest of my family was affected the way I was, whether Jacob saw things the way I was seeing them now.

All night, I tossed and turned, thinking about those weights and balloons, about truth and lies. I thought about Jacob saying what had happened wasn't right simply because we had been lied to, even if it was for our own good. What else had they lied to us about?

CHAPTER 21

The next night, Grandpa gave more of a loyalty lesson. He explained the difference between blindly following a flag, a leader, or a government into a pit of lies with patriotism as leverage, and unwaveringly following the principle that made that flag or government great – even when the flag, the government, and its followers departed from those principles. "We must not depart from them because flags come and go, and empires are built and just as quickly crumble. But the principles of liberty and freedom must be stood beside. Even if you are alone, you stand no matter the cost. We must not be terrified of what happens to us if we stand. We must be terrified of what will happen to us if we fail to stand for them."

Now I was terrified, and not for the right reason. It was as if he was telling me to abandon the system I had followed my whole life, and to cling to some principles that I didn't know existed a month ago. And to what end? If the world was on the wrong track, why was it running so well? How would just one man change things?

Like Grandpa said, laws changed, but truth was truth, and it would always be truth. As we got up to leave, he said goodbye and asked that only Jacob and I come back tomorrow. We agreed and left. Just Jacob and I? That unsettled me even further, but whatever he asked of me, I'd gladly do.

CHAPTER 22

The next night, Jacob and I headed over to see Grandpa. The conversation on the way was so lively: we discussed everything that we'd learned over the last few weeks. We were both amazed at a world we had never known existed. We went in and sat.

"Tonight's lesson is for everyone," Grandpa said. "But not from me. I will tell you, and in time you may tell them. What does evil look like?" He was very serious. "Years ago, they used to make movies about the Bible. Some were good and some were bad. Some were fairly well done, but they were all flawed in the same way: the devil."

"Um, the devil?" I muttered. "As in, the devil made me do it?"

"No," Grandpa quickly replied. "Not some cartoon guy in a red suit. The devil – Satan! Pure evil."

Jacob theorized, "I imagine he would be dark and sinister. You know, creepy and morose."

"Yes!" Grandpa shouted. "And that's how the movies portray him. But like you, they were also wrong. The devil is never dark and sinister. When he shows up, he is going to look just like your best friend. He's going to be very beautiful and extremely attractive. It's the total opposite of what logic tells us he will look like. You see, boys, God's way is always ugly and unappealing. It's tough and hard and painful. It's like your work week. You sweat and toil. You plant and you water. You wait and you wait. Then you get paid, and you can buy what you will with a clean conscience, because you earned it.

"The devil's way is easy and attractive. It's like getting credit. See, in my day, when you didn't have money, stores and other companies would give you a line of credit. You get what you want now, quickly and conveniently, and with that huge high comes instant gratification. But you end up paying much more and for much longer than you anticipated, long after what you got has lost its shine and faded away. The wrong road is going to look almost exactly like the right road. Almost. Anything God has that's good, the devil has a counterfeit, and it's going to be similar, not opposite. It's going to seem right and logical, and without God's guidance you will inevitably take that road."

We were stunned. In a short time, this man had completely uprooted our lives. "Why didn't we come to you sooner?" Jacob said.

What my grandfather said next would stay with me forever. His face turned sad, and he spoke with a quiver in his voice. "Boys, my generation is to blame for this world. You see, we had so much truth and so much freedom to serve and love God that we never took it seriously. We failed to pass on the importance of God and freedom to our children, and so slowly one was taken and the other one became obsolete. As for you boys coming to see me ..." He smiled again and softly said, "I was always here, waiting. But late or not, you did come to me."

"Yeah," I said despairingly. "But now it's too late. What can we do now?"

"It's not too late for you and your families," he said. "That's what death is for, to let you know it's too late. If you're alive, if you are here on this earth with breath in your lungs, then you can make a difference. You can be a light in a dark world."

We started to leave, but Jacob turned back. "Do you think the government was lying about the pills?"

"Yes," Grandpa said without hesitation. "They're the government. They're always lying, even when they are telling the truth. *Especially* when they're telling the truth."

As we reached the door, I looked at my grandfather differently now. "What about the third balloon? You made us bring three, but you only used two."

He smiled as he gave us both a hug. "Hey, what can I say? I like balloons."

As we rode home, I turned to Jacob and said, "Well, then. Let's go find the truth."

He quickly replied, "It's about time. This is the first time you've shown any enthusiasm. Okay, David, let's go find the truth."

CHAPTER 23

Back at the office on Monday, we had a fairly nice day with nothing too out of the ordinary. Mondays were so busy that we didn't really need to wish the day away; it flew by pretty quickly. We finished our work and locked up, and then we sat pondering. How did two relatively obscure doctors find out anything? We had no serious connections, and we had no pull, at least where the government was concerned. We certainly had no government security clearance, with the exception of ordering and prescribing medicine, and booking surgeries for our individual patients when needed – but that wasn't going to help us here. Dr McTarvish's story was very sound and very believable. The only thing keeping us from believing it completely was the fact that the drug altered users' mental state. It was only slightly, but nonetheless, they were altered. There must be a reason for altering someone's mental state. I supposed we should start there.

"Dissect the drug and find out what is in it exactly, Jacob!" I said. "Remember Nigel, with whom we went to university?"

"Nigel Lathen," he replied. "We used to call him Poncey. He was from a very posh family, and you could really tell. Last I heard, he became a druggist, running a chemist shop somewhere near Penrith. But that was years ago; he may have moved on since then. Still, I'll look him up. All the pills for the kenosis epidemic come from the government, so I imagine nobody would bother to check what's in them. Even if he is still around and we do find him, how do we ask him to dissect one and then to tell us what's in it without raising suspicion? What if he says no and reports us?"

"All good points," I said. "Unfortunately, I have no answers. All I can tell you is he's our best shot at this time."

Jacob said, "I agree. But we will have to wait a week. My petrol allowance is spent after doing all this crazy running around. I will barely be able get to work."

"Me too. In the meantime, I suggest we research this epidemic. The question is, how do we do that? After our meeting with McTarvish, we are definitely going to be flagged at work and home. We need someone else's interweb terminal and someone willing to scan in and let us …"

Tap, tap, tap. Someone was at the door.

CHAPTER 24

I walked down the long corridor from the office. Then I opened the door slightly and politely said, "We are closed."

"I'm not a patient," he replied. "I'm a friend."

"A friend of whose?" I asked.

"A friend of yours," he said, sounding very sure of himself.

I opened the door, and he strutted in looking very official. He went down the corridor as if he knew where to go, and then he sat in my chair and nonchalantly put his feet on my desk. "Dr Amiasaf and ... well, Dr Amiasaf. Perhaps in the future, I should just say Doctor Dave and Doctor Jake. Yes, I rather like the sound of that. I thought I'd pop in and say hello. I actually embellished slightly – we aren't exactly friends yet, but we do share a friend."

"Is that so?" Jacob said.

"Yes," the man answered. "The good Doctor McTarvish, of course."

"Well, um," I stammered. "We aren't actually friends with him. More, uh distant colleagues. Really just admirers of his work."

"Yes," Jacob chimed in. "Just two doctors who admire his work and the leaps he's made in modern medicine. And your relationship to him, might I inquire?"

"We work together," he answered.

"Oh, so you're a doctor, then?" I asked.

"No, not me," he quickly replied. "I could never be a doctor – don't really like dealing with all those sick people. People always whinging about this lump or that cough. No, no. I'm someone who makes sure everything runs smoothly."

"Oh, I see," said Jacob. "An office manager." It was as if he was enjoying this parry and thrust.

How could Jacob be so bold? The mere presence of this man brought this situation into reality. I was terrified. This man had a look in his eyes that could cut like a laser, like a cold, grey shark heading for its prey.

"No, not an office manager. I'm really there to make sure everything stays, well … *secure,* if you know what I mean."

"Yes, I think we do," I replied, hoping my fear wasn't too obvious. I felt as if my knees were buckling and my voice was shaking.

"Well then," Jacob said. "How can we help you this afternoon, Mr …?"

"Tarlick. Chief Security Inspector Tarlick," he said.

Now I was sure of it. I was genuinely terrified. "Well, CSI Tarlick, how can my brother and I avail ourselves to you today?"

"Oh, no way at all, really. This is not an official visit. On the contrary, this is just a visit between friends. Although we just met, I'm hoping for a long and illustrious friendship. Maybe not the kind where I'm over for dinner a whole lot, but certainly the kind where we encourage each other to do the right thing when faced with difficult decisions. For instance, you two signed an agreement the other day saying that you would not discuss whatever it is you think you discovered. I could not call myself a good friend if I didn't encourage you to keep that agreement, could I?"

"No, I suppose you couldn't. But then you will be very happy, friend," Jacob responded. "Because we have kept our part quite happily. Right, David?"

"Oh, yes, quite happily," I said. "We don't even talk about it to each other. It's all but forgotten."

"That's wonderful," Tarlick said cheerfully. "Then I shall be on my way." He quickly he got up and made his way to the door. "I'll be seeing you," he said as he stepped down to the sidewalk.

"Will you?" I enquired.

"Well, you know, with us being friends and all that. I'm more than certain we will be wanting to keep in touch from time to time. Good day." With that, he casually strolled down the sidewalk and around the corner. I locked the door and went back in to Jacob.

"Wasn't he supposed to threaten us?" Jacob said smugly.

"What?" I replied.

"You know, as he was leaving. He was suppose to say something like, 'You have a nice practice here. Pity if anything was to happen to it.' Or mentioning our addresses or kids' names. You know, the ominous threat laced nicely inside of a pleasantry."

"He didn't bleedin' have to!" I shouted. "It was understood! I am quite sure that he has everything, every single piece of information on us, right down to that bed-wetting problem you had when you were five. And if he was a good judge of body language, he would also know I was about to develop a wetting problem of my own. Now, perhaps when these situations arise, you get a rush of adrenaline and feel all heaven and earth move, and the angels sing. But I just have a desire to wet myself and fall onto the floor in the fetal position. I am just not cut out for this."

"I know," Jacob replied quietly. "I'm scared too."

"What do we do? Do we forget it?"

"No, we don't forget it. But I do think we should let it cool. Let's wait for a while."

CHAPTER 25

The beginning of a new month arrived, and then another and another. Life was business as usual: seeing our patients, doing our paperwork, and keeping our minds busy. That worked fine for me during the day, but each night my mind wandered endlessly. Every night I lay in bed thinking, theorizing. This machine that had changed so many lives for the better was also holding us hostage. Then there was that pill that cured nothing but mildly tranquilized users. The only place they gave drugs to subdue your drive and your emotions was in facilities for the mentally unstable – people who didn't have or were unable to use their full reasoning capabilities, to keep them and others around them safe from harm.

But the world? We weren't a danger to anyone. I'd never spent a minute in a mental facility. Well, I had but as a physician, but not a patient. The dosage wasn't near what they gave the patients in those places, but it did take some of the aggression out of people. That was something I wasn't even capable of realizing until I was off it for a week, and even then, others had to point it out. But once off it, I was much more interested in finding out the truth of this mystery. While on it, I didn't care.

David's aggression off the pill was far more intense than mine. He'd been the driving factor behind getting us this far. My fears far outweighed my aggression. My eyes must have been so bloodshot from all these nights of late thinking. I couldn't remember the last time I'd had a normal night's sleep. I wondered if I'd ever get one again.

Tomorrow was the day we set on the calendar to start discussing this situation again, and how we should proceed. The day was hard to pass. I was full of anticipation about the meeting and wasn't sure what we would decide, but I was anxious to move forward.

We locked up as usual. "Do you have a plan?" Jacob said.

"Me? I thought you had a plan."

"Well, it seems like one of us is going to go see Ponce – Nigel."

"Yes," I replied. "I can do that. I have a death gap."

A death gap was an opening in the patient schedule that came when patients passed away and the government had not yet assigned new patients to replace them. Technology hadn't sped up the bureaucratic process in government by any means; they worked at the same speed as they did in the days of scrolls and quills.

"How big a gap?" Jacob asked.

I said, "I lost two patients last week, and one was reassigned to Grandpa's facility. That's a three-patient gap. I could shuffle enough to give me a full day off, if I'm canny."

"Do it."

We decided that I would go to Penrith to see Nigel. I shelved the nickname because I recalled he didn't much care for it. Jacob had a friend from our primary school days, he believed the friend would allow him use of an information terminal. Jacob and I traded comm devices in the hopes that we could communicate without symptoms.

CHAPTER 26

It was a very pleasant ride to Penrith. I arrived and started asking around, to try to find as many druggist shops as possible. Of course, everyone said the exact same thing: "Why don't you use the map app on your personal communication device?" I didn't want to because that would be a traceable search. I was doing it the ancient way, on foot.

After a few inquiries, someone finally said Nigel was their druggist, and I quickly got an address. I arrived and went in. Nigel was there, and as luck would have it, no one else was. I quickly told him who I was, and he remembered me and my brother. We exchanged pleasantries, but then I told him of my time constraints. He was puzzled but was glad to see me after so long. We went to his counter.

"So I'm at a loss," he said. "I mean, everyone knows what's in these pills. It's on the package. What I mean is every ingredient *has* to be on the package. Putting anything in a pharmaceutical product without listing it on the label is illegal."

"Yes," I replied, "but just humour me here. Jacob and I have a little bet going that there's an ingredient in there that isn't on the package. I told him everything you just told me, but he insisted, and you know Jacob."

"Good ol' Jacob!" Nigel said. "How is he? Boy, I tell you. That little brother of yours was such a mess for such a genius."

"What?" I said. "Jacob's not my little brother. I'm his little brother. He was two years ahead of me in university. Didn't that tip you off?"

"Oh, no, not at all," Nigel replied. "Jacob said he was so smart that he was skipped ahead several years."

"Skipped ahead!" I repeated. "If I hadn't helped him through chemistry, he would still be in school!"

"That is just like Jacob," he said.

"Yes, actually, it is," I replied.

Nigel said, "I just thought you were aging really well."

"Nope, I'm almost three years his junior."

"Well, this will take a few days. I'll give you a call."

"No! Uh, I mean, I would really like to find out before Jacob does, so I'll just come back. How's Thursday?"

"Thursday should be fine," he assured me. "You know, your brother and his mates used to call me Poncey because they thought I was a blue blood."

"Poncey?" I said with a really dumb look on my face. "That's new to me. I never heard that."

CHAPTER 27

I left Nigel and headed home. I hoped our suspicions were wrong. If we were right, it would open up a million more questions. It was a pleasant drive with just me and my thoughts. What was all this leading to? Why bother with all this epidemic stuff? I mean, if it was not for the reasons of economics and pharmaceutical companies, as Dr McTarvish had indicated, then what else was left?

This was so surreal. I was such an insignificant person, not even a blip on life's radar. If not for an accident with my communication device, I'd be living life as normal. Of course, Grandpa would disagree. "There are no accidents with God," he said to me and Jacob while we were with him. But if Grandpa's God was real, what did he want with me? How could I possibly fit into such a big picture? These thoughts ran through my head on a continuous loop. Perhaps I believed subconsciously that if I kept dwelling on it, the answer would jump out at me. Wishful thinking, but it couldn't hurt to go over it a lot; maybe I was missing something.

I arrived back at the office and went in. Jacob was waiting. "What was in the drug?" he said.

"Nothing," I replied.

"You didn't call him Poncey, did you?"

"Of course not. He's not upset; it's simply going to take a bit of time, so we won't have the results until Thursday. I have to drive back. But I did find out you're a genius who excelled so much that he was two years ahead of his older brother at university."

"What? Oh, right." He giggled like an evil mastermind. "I thought you knew about that. Actually, I only said it to get Janey Halen to go out with me, but it spread so quickly, and then the ladies came out of the woodwork, so I rode it out. Pretty clever, huh?" He was grinning like the Cheshire cat.

What could I say? Janey Halen was the most beautiful girl on campus, and everyone thought Jacob was going to marry her. But life was funny that way. "Yeah, I suppose it was a pretty crazy stunt," I said reluctantly. "And what about you? Did your research turn up anything?"

"I actually did find a few things. I do work when you're not here, you know."

"I never said otherwise. I think it sometimes, but I would never say it."

CHAPTER 28

Jacob continued. "It turns out that the root word for the kenosis epidemic, *kenosis,* is an old Greek or Hebrew word that means an emptying of one's own self and a heightened receptiveness to the will of a higher power – God's will, for example. Why would you name an epidemic for that?"

"Not a clue," I replied.

"I also cross-referenced the rise in social behaviour and the rise in prescription drug use."

"Why would you do that? I mean, what difference does that make?"

"Just my gut," he replied. "Did you know that before the beginning of the twentieth century, society was pretty normal? But then there came a wave of doctors giving every single quirk or behavioural trait a name. Not too many years after that came the medication, and lots of it. Then it got into the legal system. It seems that anytime someone got into trouble of any kind, they were stuck into a category and given a prescription as part of their sentence."

"What's the point?" I asked. "I mean, how does that fit into what we are looking for?"

"Well, as they were diagnosing all these new 'illnesses' and treating them, society was getting worse. By the time the twenty-first century rolled around, a massive percentage of the population was on some kind of mood drug or such."

"Still, how does that relate to us?"

"Stick with me, big brother. I'm going somewhere with this." Jacob said with a smirk.

"Listen, lunatic. If you call me your big brother again, you are going to need a prescription of some kind."

"Okay, okay. We needed a theory, and this is mine. As I was saying, it seems to me that through the years, governments were trying individually to get as many people on some kind of mood-altering drugs as they could. This way, they had a logical and viable reason to deny them things that people believed were God-given rights for all humans, such as voting or owning firearms. The governments got a huge amount of people on them, but not nearly enough, and certainly not everyone. But an epidemic? That would be the perfect vehicle to sedate the whole planet."

"But for what intent or purpose?" I said. "I mean, people shouldn't own dangerous weapons. I'm glad they got rid of them, and only duly appointed agents of the government should be armed. That cannot be the only reason that everyone needs to be sedated."

"I don't know," Jacob replied. "I haven't quite figured that out yet. But what if we are wrong? What if Grandpa is right? What if unrest in society was a result of government interference and a decline in religious beliefs? You know, a decline in the teaching of morality in relation to a higher power?"

I said, "Jacob, we have been taught since birth to pledge allegiance to the government, to be loyal. We've built our lives on that."

"You asked me for a theory, and this is it."

"You found this all on the web?"

"No, this stuff is from old books I found in Dad's attic. I tried finding it on the web, but the search got flagged, and I got spooked. I went to Dad's and rifled through his attic. His early curriculum school books were real paper books, and he still had them. I read until my eyes hurt and then filled my car with them. There was no way I could finish. I say we split them and finish them separately at home."

I replied, "Yeah, that should help my marital relations. They're not idiots – they know something is going on. They're patient, but there's a breaking point. And what about our comm devices? Do we continue using each other's?"

"I think if we kept the batteries out, we could trade back," Jacob replied. "Just put a message on your answer phone asking people to contact you here at the office. I'll do the same."

"That sounds fine to me," I replied.

CHAPTER 29

The next few days consisted of a lot of thinking. Jacob's idea was so insane when I first heard it, but as the days ticked by, it seemed much more plausible and sensible.

I was brought quickly from a daydream by the office phone ringing. It was Rachael. She said, "Grandpa wants to see you and Jacob tonight."

I told Jacob, and after we closed, we headed over to the pensioners facility. I could tell Jacob's mind was racing faster than mine. He had a theory and was desperate to prove it. We walked in and took the lift to Grandpa's floor. I looked up at the camera in the lift and thought, *Wow. It's amazing how you can't unlearn things. I mean, a year ago, I only saw my own life, and it seemed quite private. Now I notice all these technological devices everywhere: the personal communication devices, the information terminals, the cameras. All the bloomin' cameras. They are everywhere and always have been, but I never noticed them. Now I can't help but notice them, and I feel them. There is no private place anywhere, only your own mind.*

We exited the lift and headed down the corridor very slowly, it seemed. Or maybe the corridor simply seemed longer today. We knocked, and Grandpa came to the door. We went in and sat, and he made us cups of tea. He asked what was new. I told him my conniving brother had pulled a huge scam at university and told everyone he was skipped ahead in school four years because he was a genius. Grandpa laughed so hard that I thought he was going to die. "I thought you would yell at him," I said, stunned.

"Yell at him?" he said. "Who do you think gave him the idea?"

"You told him?"

"Yep. I did the same thing when I was at university," Grandpa said, still grinning.

"But what about all that stuff about doing right and telling the truth?" I chastised.

"Well I wasn't always a God-fearing man, David. I was quite the handful in my younger days. Anyway, I had to come up with a way of getting Charlene Hendricks's attention. She was so beautiful."

"Great," I replied. "So Great Uncle Isaac and I get the royal boot for two women neither of you two married."

"No. Isaac went into service. It was your Great Uncle Charles I pulled that one on. And by the by, things went his way eventually. He ended up marrying her, and they were very happy together for many years. Unfortunately, they both died in a plane crash years later. But they were happy, and they were together. I sure wish your grandmother was here now. I miss her. She was a very special woman, boys."

Jacob replied, "I still remember all those desserts she would bring over when we were children."

"Yes," Grandpa replied. "She loved to bake. It broke her heart when they started the rationing. But still she managed to save enough to make you boys a little something every month."

"Well, I don't suppose you called us here to discuss Grandma's baking," Jacob noted.

"No, boys, I didn't."

CHAPTER 30

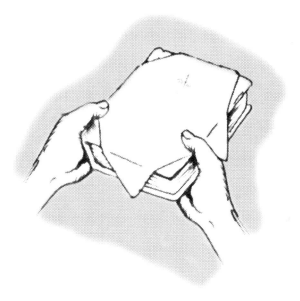

Grandpa's face became steely. "I have a couple of things to say – important things. I need you to listen closely. A few hundred years ago, a war broke out between two great nations. Well, at least they used to be great. Anyway, the colonies were feeling that their viewpoints and beliefs weren't being represented properly, and if they were to be a part of this empire, they deserved representatives and fair treatment. As the war progressed, they were struggling, and it looked as if they weren't going to win, at least not without help. They teamed up with the French."

"We already know all of this, Grandpa," I said.

"I know, son, but just listen," he replied with a very strong yearning in his voice. "You see, after the war, a bond appeared to be formed between the two countries. The French wanted to give the colonists a gift, so they commissioned at statue to be built. That's how the Americans ended up with the Statue of Liberty."

"You mean the Lady of the Harbour, don't you, Grandpa?"

"Yes, but they have only called her that for about thirty years. Before that, she was called Lady Liberty, to symbolize freedom from tyranny and oppression. You see, the war wasn't against Britain. Most people loved the homeland. It was against the principles of tyranny. We also fought wars for this purpose, because it's against our nature to be under a dictator. But I'm getting off-track. The point is when forming their government, this new country needed a system of laws, and they had two choices: the law system in the country that aided them, or the country they had just left – French civil law or British common law. Logic would of course lead us to believe they chose the law of their ally, not their enemy, but they didn't. They chose the law of their enemy, and here's why.

"First, they understood that French civil law said that if you educated people, then intelligent people can make intelligent decisions. British common law stated that there is an absolute, and we should adhere to it. There is a right, and there is a wrong, and right must be followed. Figuring things out does not simply solve problems. Reason two: these two nations were part of a much bigger plan, and a temporary spat did not make them enemies. They are forever linked through things bigger than the understanding of mortal men. These things were talked about by the prophet Daniel, but the interpretation of his prophesies were not revealed to him during his life.

"Now, these countries are referred to by the prophet, by the animals that represent them. Britain has always been referred to as a lion, because the lion is king, and through the years we have had the most famous monarchy in history. America is represented by the eagle. This book even goes so far as to say that the eagle came out from the lion, showing the history that one nation was formed from out of the other. However, they are referred to singularly as one entity. These prophesies are later brought to light in a book called the Revelation of Jesus Christ, as written by his servant John. This book speaks of the end of the world and how in the times to come, many things have to come together and line up. After this, there is an almost perfect world formed, but an artificial temporary perfect world. In an instant, evil men turn against God."

"What happens to the two great nations?" I asked.

"I'm old, and I have some wisdom, but I am by no means a prophet. I don't know what happens to those two nations, because it hasn't happened yet. What I mean is whatever happens is happening right now – we are living it. We are part of these end days, and at some time, things are going to get very bad. You see, the world will get better, and cunning men will solve most of the problems, including the age-old fight between Isaac and Ishmael. But make no mistake: these men cannot be trusted, and they are no friends of our father Isaac. After the accord is broken, things fall apart quickly: there are plagues, meteors, and earthquakes, as well as the four horsemen of the apocalypse."

"Four horsemen?" I said, confused by what he was saying.

"Yes, the four horsemen. Death, famine, pestilence, and Ric Flair." Grandpa chuckled loudly. "Ric Flair – get it? Oh, never mind. Kids these days! It's just something my mates and I used to say in Sunday school. Anyway, boys, it's important that you remember that these once-great nations based their laws on God's word, and there was a time that the leaders of these nations had respect for God and held high his word. When that stopped, greatness faded. But most important, always remember that God has a plan. You two are part of that plan, and in order to fulfil it, you will need this."

Grandpa pulled an old box from under his bed and carefully

opened it. He pulled out something large and rectangular wrapped in tattered cloth. Then he handed it to me and sternly said, "Cherish this, boys. This is what made those nations great, and it holds all the answers to life."

"Thank you, Grandpa. We will," I replied.

CHAPTER 31

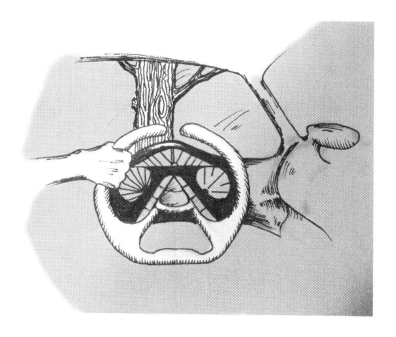

"Now, boys, as you know, in a few months I turn eighty-five."

"Eighty-five? Is that so?" Jacob said, acting aloof. He knew our dad was planning a big get-together.

"Yes, eighty-five. The council has alerted me that they will be allotting this space and medicine to someone else – someone more productive. You're both doctors, and you know how it works."

"Yes, but without your medicine ... I mean, well ..."

I knew what was going on. It happened all the time. It was a part of life. Honestly, a few months back, I would have taken it in stride, but that was before we got to know this incredible man and his knowledge of life and supernatural things. He still had so much life left in him. We didn't say much and knew grandpa wouldn't want us troubling ourselves about it. We would be very troubled, but not now – not in front of him.

When we got into the car, we headed home in silence at first.

"Jacob?" I finally said.

"Yeah?"

"What's a Ric Flair?"

"I have no idea," he answered. "I was wondering that myself. Must be some religious term for famine or death, or something."

It was quiet again for a few moments, and then suddenly Jacob blurted, "Fiends! Those evil, maniacal fiends! He's not even sick!"

"We fiends," I replied.

"What?"

"We fiends, Jacob. Not those fiends. We are the evil, maniacal fiends. Up until a few months ago, we were perfectly willing to be soulless minions of the mindless nirvana. It's our fault. How could we be so blind? Such lemmings – and not just us, but everyone."

Jacob interjected. "The worst part is that all of this could have been prevented by people sitting and listening to their grandpas. It's not like … Ahh, uhh!" Jacob stammered, and his head lurched back as he slammed his foot to the floor.

"What is it?" I shrieked. He started shaking violently and was turning red in the face. He was choking, and we were speeding. "What is it, Jake? Hey, Jakey, talk to me!"

He had a death grip on the steering wheel and was having some kind of seizure. I tried desperately to pry his hands from the wheel. We were in trouble, and I had no idea what to do. "Jacob, please!" I screamed. "Try to get your foot off the accelerator. We need to stop. We are going to crash!" He was shaking uncontrollably more and more. I was terrified out of my mind. I had no idea whether Jacob was going to die from what was happening to him, but I was sure we both would die if I didn't stop this car. It had been on auto drive, and he hadn't even been driving, but when the seizure hit, he instinctively grabbed the wheel, and now I couldn't get him off.

I fumbled frantically with my safety belt, but it was locked. The more I fumbled, the harder it became. I was trapped! I had to get free to get over to Jacob. I could see the scenery zooming by the houses, and trees were a blur. I had no idea what the speed was, but it must have been seventy or eighty. I had to slow down and cautiously get this safety belt off. Fumbling in a panic wasn't going to get it done. I stopped and simply pressed the button firmly. There was nothing at first, but then it popped. I was free! I was facing Jacob, but now I was backwards in the car. I put my foot over the centre console.

"Jacob, please forgive me," I cried. I reared back my leg and closed my eyes. With all my might, I kicked his leg off the accelerator. I was straddling the centre console backwards, trying to feel for the brake pedal and trying to hold on to Jacob so he didn't choke to death. "I can't find it, I can't find it. I just ruddy well can't find it!" The scenery was speeding by faster and faster as I desperately tried to hold on to Jacob and find that brake. I was drenched in sweat and tears, and the salt stung my eyes. I was trying to grasp the wheel so I could steer, but I still couldn't find that brake. Finally, I got it. I hit the brake pedal with all my might, trying to get the car to stop before we died. As I pushed, I could feel it might be too late. The drive suddenly got very bumpy, and we were being jolted all around the inside of car. We were off the road and heading up a hill. My head was pounding, and adrenaline was surging. Suddenly, everything went black …

CHAPTER 32

There was blackness. There was a buzz inside my head like a sawmill, or like standing inside a huge machine at an industrial compound. I was not asleep, but I was not quite awake. I had no idea if I was dead or alive, but I was fairly certain that at some point, an elephant had stood on my head. I could feel the pounding and thumping.

I desperately tried to put my head back into focus, but I couldn't. I had no idea what was going on. The pain behind my eyes was so severe, and I knew opening them was probably the last thing I should do, but I needed to. I slowly opened my eyes, and everything was blurry.

"Hi there," someone said. The voice was familiar.

"Rachael?" I murmured. "Is that you? What happened?"

"I'm right here, handsome," she said as she grabbed my hand. Now I knew it was her; she always called me handsome.

"Is there an elephant on my head?: I mumbled.

"Oh, baby. Is that what it feels like? No, love, they got rid of the elephant at the crash scene – although technically, it was a windscreen."

"Tell me where Jacob is," I said. I still wasn't very clear, and I wasn't exactly sure, but I really wanted to see Jacob.

"Jacob is fine," she replied.

"What happened? I mean, what happened to us? It was all such a blur."

"Apparently the car stopped in time to not damage it too badly, but it did set off the air restraints, one of which hit you in the back off the head, knocked you into the glass, and rendered you unconscious."

"And Jacob?"

"Nobody knows what caused it, but he had some kind of seizure. He is down the hall and should be fine. He just got out of surgery."

"Surgery!" I yelled. "For what? Why? What happened to him that he needed surgery?"

Rachael squeezed my hand. "They said he cut his hand. That's all I know. It was emergency surgery, and they didn't have time to tell us everything. Really, my handsome, he'll be all right. Please get some rest, and you'll be home by morning."

I was very groggy, and everything she was saying seemed so distant. Either from the hit to my head or the medicine, I was slipping into the dark. I closed my eyes and drifted off. I felt Rachael kiss me, and then nothing …

CHAPTER 33

Silence. Sweet, soft silence, with the occasional interruption of a soft blip from the medical scanner in the room ... Was I dreaming? I thought I was, but I could see the street light coming through the window and the light in the hallway shining under the door. There was a soft green glow coming from the medical scanner readout. My eyes adjusted, and I wiggled my fingers and looked at my arms. I was not hooked to anything. I didn't suppose any alarms would sound if I got out of bed for a moment. I needed to see Jacob. I may be drugged and hazy, but I was fine.

I thought about getting to his room for a minute. I'd never formulated a "getting out of bed" plan before. I had some doubts about the logistics of it, but I was fairly certain would be there. I twisted my body towards the side of the bed and put my feet onto the floor, which was very cold. I was right about the pain. How could *everything* hurt? I'd never dreamed the human body could be so sore. I grabbed the rail and made a push. I was up.

"Careful, now. You've had a rough day," a voice said from the darkness.

"Who's there?" I said.

"Just a friend," he replied. "Here to take care of you. I heard you and Jacob had a bit of an accident." That voice was familiar, but the lights were dimmed. "You know, you two have to be more careful. A *lot* more careful."

Now I was sure of who it was. That scary security inspector. So much for thinking my night had bottomed out. "Yes," I replied. "I suppose we do, Chief Security Inspector Tarleck. I guess we're just gluttons for punishment."

"Interesting choice of words there. Punishment. I hear Jacob had a seizure of some kind. Terrible, just terrible," he said unremorsefully. "It's probably stress related. Yes, stress. I'm sure of it. Stress will kill you, you know. If I were you two, I would cut back on the unimportant things and concentrate on work and family. Trim the fat, get rid of all those extra things that stress you out. Who needs it? That's what I always say. Who needs it? I wouldn't want to see anymore of these accidents happen – or worse."

Thank goodness it was dark, or else this horrible man would be able to see me shaking uncontrollably. I was such a coward. This guy genuinely put a fear into me that was like nothing I'd ever felt. But I had to be strong. I had to be more like Jacob.

"Do you like your job, CSI Tarleck?" I asked.

"Do I like my job?" he repeated, sounding puzzled.

I was in now, so I may as well push on. "Yes, exactly. Do you like your job?"

"I love my job," he replied, sounding extremely sure of himself. "Why do you ask?"

"No reason. "You just seem so … Well, forget it. I'm just glad you enjoy what you do. If you want to hang around, CSI Tarleck, you may. My bed pan is ready, and I was thinking about maybe throwing up in a bit. That's probably going to be exciting. But for now, I'm going to see my brother. I'll see you later, friend."

I couldn't believe I'd just said that to him, especially the bed pan bit. I'd just thought of it. Of course, it was all an act. If he even motioned like he was coming my way, I would fall over and scream a lot. The coldness in this man's eyes terrified me something wicked.

CHAPTER 34

Now, to get to the door, I thought. It must have been a hundred miles away, but I was on the move. Shuffling was not an incredibly speedy form of travel, but it was getting the job done. I eventually made it to the door. I knew the nurses would rush me right back to bed, so I had to sneak out of the room, find Jacob's room, and get into it without getting caught – all while in a drug-induced fog. Shouldn't be too hard.

I pushed the door open just enough to peek out. Why were hospital doors so heavy? This was like moving a boulder. I could only see one way, but it was clear. I stepped lightly into the corridor and started my hallway shuffle. *I'm going to make it,* I thought.

"And just where do you think you're going?" a sharp voice said.

Not even two steps, and I'm caught. Typical of my night. "I need to see my brother," I replied as I turned around.

"Not tonight," the nurse said very calmly. "Anyway, he's sleeping." She seemed stern but had very kind eyes. It was hard to explain, but this nurse put me at ease. I didn't know whether she had a soft spot, but I was going to assume she did, and I pleaded to her sense of family.

"Please," I said. "I don't need to talk to him I just need to see him. Please? Five minutes. I won't be a bother."

She replied, "Hmm. I knew the moment I saw you, you would be trouble."

"Not me. I'm a kitten – a soft, fluffy kitten."

She lowered her eyebrows. "Well, I should march you right back to bed, but I suppose some things are too important to put off till tomorrow."

"Cheers," I mumbled.

I took a few steps and stumbled slightly, but then I felt something steady and strong under my arm.

"You really are going to make this a long night for me, aren't you?" Nurse Graham said.

"Yes," I replied. "It looks as though I'm going to be quite a burden."

"All right. Lean on me. I'll get you there," she said in a soft, firm voice. She walked me to the end of the corridor.

"Thanks, Nurse Graham. I can get it from here."

"Okay, kitten. You've got two minutes, and not a second more. Don't disturb him."

"Oh, no. I wouldn't disturb anyone."

She looked as if she didn't believe me, but she turned and headed back to the nurses' station. "Five minutes past four, Doctor. That's the time at this moment," she said as she walked away.

I shuffled around the corner, thinking about Nurse Graham. I saw people so differently now. What kind of person would she be if she wasn't on the kenosis pill? What if her life was not so structured? I used to love structure, living a life I could set my watch by, perfectly tuned, predictable, boring, controlled. Ah, yes – controlled. Perfectly controlled by the state. It was funny how all this stuff was constantly going through my head. It never used to. I couldn't get over that. We were a world full of drones. Jacob was right about it all, and now because of me, he was in a hospital bed, unconscious.

CHAPTER 35

I was soon at his door. After that quick shuffle, I was a bit lightheaded. I steadied myself against the door frame and slowly pushed open the door. It was dark, and I crept in. Jacob looked fine – no visible damage beside his right hand. It was bandaged from the cut Rachael said he had received from the car crash. I sat there, staring.

"Hi, David," a voice said out of the darkness.

I nearly jumped out of my skin. "Who is that?" I thought, "Please tell me there's not another thug in here watching Jacob."

"It's me, Gabriellah. I couldn't leave him, so Michael is at your house with Rachael."

I was so relieved to hear a friendly voice – one that didn't terrify me as it came out of the shadows.

She said, "David, how could this happen? I mean, you're a doctor. How does a perfectly healthy man have a seizure?"

Well ..." I paused to say it right. "I think the government did this. I just can't figure out how."

"Dear Lord," she cried. "It's my fault."

"Your fault? How exactly could this be your fault?"

"I asked Jacob to take his communication device – with the battery out, of course, so he could call to say he was leaving to head home. I worry so much since this all started. He was supposed to call and then take the battery back out, but when the nurse gave me his belongings, his comm device was still on. It's because of me."

"I'm guessing Jacob filled you in on some details. We agreed not to involve you two – not because we didn't want to, but because we were so worried about what any of us knew. We figured if you and Rachael didn't know anything then you could say that you knew nothing without lying. Anyway, Gabriellah, it's most certainly not your fault. Jacob and I knew the risks. It's somebody's fault for sure, but not yours."

"Using mobile communication devices to create serious injury if people don't do as you wish is tyranny, or so Grandpa says. It was a tyranny I was very content to live under, because I didn't know it existed. Even after I knew, I wasn't going to do much. It was Jacob who had the courage to stand. I drew my courage from him, and I need him to be okay."

"Me too," Gabriellah said. "You're right, David. Jacob is strong – but so are you. Jacob may help bring it out of you, but he couldn't bring it out if it wasn't there. He draws a lot of strength from you too. Maybe it's not immediately evident, but it's true. He tells me that you encourage him to be more, to see this thing to the end. Don't be upset with him, David. I was a mess and pleaded with him to tell me why he refused to take his personal communication device. He really was strong, but I begged. David, I do see your reasoning, and certainly you can argue that it's the correct line of thinking. But try to see this from our point of view. Rachael and I are seeing you two go through this drastic change, which you are both trying so desperately to hide. But we know, we see. We talk to each other because we're your wives. We're in already, so let us in. Tell Rachael."

"I see why he told you. You're quite the persuader. I'd better get back to my room." I said. "There's a nurse out there granting me a spot of graciousness, and I get the feeling I had better not abuse it. Besides, I'm a bit weak just now. Good night, Gabriellah. Take care of my brother."

CHAPTER 36

I crept back down the corridor and could see my gracious benefactor sitting at her desk. I slipped by quietly. She looked up from her terminal with a raised eyebrow and spoke softly. "I trust I won't have any more trouble out of you tonight, will I, kitten?" I smiled at her in gratitude and shook my head. "Get some rest, Doctor."

Absolutely no argument here, I thought. Back in my room I was wide wake with lots of time to think. CSI Tarleck was gone – at least, I thought he was gone. Why would I ask him if he liked his job? Did I really think I could plant a seed that what he was doing was wrong? I supposed I did. Well, I got my answer: he immensely enjoyed his job. *It's a funny thing about power. We think we will do so much good once we get it, but then when we get it, we realize we don't need to do any good with it, so we wield it like a sword, flailing it around wherever and whenever we want, not caring who it may cut – and sometimes even cutting on purpose.* Jacob and I did it, making surgical or treatment recommendations based on data on a sheet of paper. "Is he young enough? Is she strong enough? Are they valuable enough to be worth the resources?" We'd used position and power, played God, and patted ourselves on the back for our practical decisions and precise management of the government's resources.

People are not numbers, statistics, or data. People were people, and they mattered – all of them. We took an oath to do no harm, but we sent the elderly to be liquidated because we thought they'd burden society. We terminated pregnancies if the fetus showed any sign of being invalid. We played God, but we were not gods.

I never knew my head could hurt so much. I was so very sleepy. The thoughts in my head were still swirling, but randomly now; ideas were falling apart as fatigue forced its way in and ordered a complete shutdown. The darkness actually felt good now …

CHAPTER 37

The next morning came quickly. I felt like I'd just closed my eyes. It was rainy today, and a little grey. I felt much better. It was amazing what some sleep could do for the body and mind. I could almost convince myself that my visitor last night was a horrible, drug-induced nightmare.

The door opened, and I heard a beautiful voice. "Time to get going." Rachael walked in with the kids. "Ready to go?"

"Am I ever," I replied. "How's Jake?"

"He's up and about, and also ready to leave."

"Well, then, let's go."

We went into the hall and headed towards the nurses' station. Jacob was already there, looking very good. "Hi, Davey boy," he said cheerfully. "Next time, you drive."

"You got it, Jake-o-lantern," I replied.

We hadn't used those nicknames for years. It was funny how when we got hurt, we turned back into children.

"Let's go," Gabriellah said. We all turned to walk out.

"Hang on," I said. "I forgot something." I went back to the desk.

The nurse looked up. "Yes, Doctor? May I help you?"

"Yes. Tell Nurse Graham I said thanks."

"Nurse Graham? I don't think I know her," she replied.

"Well, maybe I misread her name badge. But you know – the thin, pleasant-looking young nurse who worked the desk last night? The one with the kind eyes?"

"Doctor, we were short-staffed last night, so I came in to cover. It was only me and Nurse Cranston behind the desk here."

"You didn't see me talking to her at my door last night?" I asked.

"No, sir," she replied. "I saw you come out and walk down the corridor to your brother's room, but you were alone."

"Never mind," I said. "Have a nice day."

As I left, I thought how funny it was that in a building that never slept, so many people could sit at the same station and never meet at all, because they worked different shifts or different areas. I caught up with my family, and they were waiting for me at the lift. I told Jacob I'd see him in the morning, and we headed home. I kept thinking about what Gabriellah had said. I supposed I should tell Rachael what all this was about. I owed it to her.

The next morning, I slowly got dressed and headed downstairs. Rachael was waiting with a cup of tea. She said, "Dear, couldn't you take one day off to recover? I happen to know that as we speak, Gabriellah is convincing Jacob to stay home."

"Don't you think I know that?" I replied. "We're wise to you, missy. I happen to know that right know, Jacob has all his defences up. We have to go to work. I'm fine, really. I'm sore and achy, but I really do feel like I can make it through. Plus, we haven't had time to notify our patients. I promise if I'm not fine, I'll come home, climb into bed, and whinge and complain the rest of the day." Rachael smiled reluctantly, but that was all I needed. Her smile was the best medicine I could ever receive.

CHAPTER 38

We were back at work and back to normal. Not the old normal, but the new normal, which was anything but normal. Every day, we got deeper and deeper into this thing, whatever this thing was. Was it a search for truth? Was it a mission to find corruption, or to right some wrongs? Maybe it was a fundamental change in our beliefs and lives. I didn't know. All I did know was that my head hurt. I couldn't imagine how Jacob must feel – everything I felt, plus seizures for the entire ride.

We didn't see many patients today, and we agreed to go light for a week or so. If Jacob was hurting, he hid it well. He didn't look miserable and didn't complain. We managed to make it through the day.

"I'm locking up," Jacob shouted.

"Go home," I yelled. "I'll lock up."

I heard the door shut and leaned back in my chair. It was a real effort to get up.

Jacob came around the corner. "Let's brainstorm," he said.

"Are you kidding? You just went through the ruddy wringer. I mean, you genuinely look like ... well, you don't look good, I'll tell you that. You must feel terrible. *Go home.* We can talk in a few days. There's no rush. You are hurt. Trust me – I'm a doctor."

He paused, took a breath, and looked at me very seriously. Then he smiled ever so slightly. "I am all those things. Yes, I'm hurting.

My face feels … well, like it looks. My body feels worse. I'm nervous and worried. I'm scared, but I'm excited too. I'm extremely excited."

"Me too. Who wouldn't be? I mean, car crashes are just the tip of the proverbial iceberg. If we play our cards right, maybe some government-trained no-necks will beat us up tomorrow. Oh, and the next day, a bomb in the car. And the next day, a bleedin' gun to the back of the skull."

"Okay, okay," he said. "I'm not saying it hasn't been crazy and dangerous and scary, but we are getting somewhere. Obviously, I'm not excited about being almost killed, but for the first time in my life, I'm finding out what life is about: truth and purpose. I'm hungry for this stuff. I want to see Grandpa and hear everything, and I want to make things right. I don't just need to atone – I genuinely want to atone. I want to live a life with purpose. And if that life is shorter because of some government-paid hooligan with an unquenchable thirst for blood, so be it. So, brother, are you with me?"

I replied, "Well, I really just want some comfortable shoes. These ones are killing me."

"What?"

"Of course I'm with you. I have to be now, after that speech. I'd be teary-eyed if my tear ducts weren't swollen shut from trying to shove them though a plate glass windscreen. Where did you get that from? You know, you should write that down. Atone? That is a hundred-pound word. Who says *atone* anymore?"

"I thought you'd like that. Anyway, *atone* is a very fitting word."

"Okay, keep atone in the speech and go home. I'm in all the way, but we can brainstorm tomorrow. I'm exhausted. Besides, now that you've taken it upon yourself to include your wife, I need to do the same. I need a slow ride home so I can figure out how to properly word my speech."

"Yeah, it's not easy coming up with a good 'your whole life is a lie' speech. And you were quite right earlier: I really am hurting. Hey! Perhaps you can work in the word *atone*."

"I was thinking of *amends*. Doesn't that sound good?" I said.

"That's a great idea," he replied. "*Amends* is fantastic. Go with that. Of course, it's no *atone*."

We locked up and went home. I didn't tell him about our "friend" paying me a visit. I wasn't sparing him or anything like that. So much was happening, and there really hadn't been a good time. I'd fill him in later. Not that I completely understood the visit myself. *Let him have a night's sleep without worrying.*

CHAPTER 39

Morning came, and I headed to work. As I pulled up, Jacob was just arriving, and he looked refreshed.

"Morning, mate," I said. "Are you feeling better?"

"I have a warm feeling in my heart," he replied.

We went to unlock the door but noticed it was already unlocked. "Now *there* is something to warm the heart," I said. "Chloea beating us to work!"

"Good morning, Chloea," Jacob yelled down the corridor.

"Good morning, doctors," came the reply in a deep, terribly familiar voice.

"That warm feeling just left my heart," Jacob said.

"Mine too," I replied as we rounded the corner. Our fears were confirmed.

"Miss me?" CSI Tarleck inquired.

"Not in the slightest," Jacob mumbled.

"What can we do for you, Chief Security Inspector Tarleck?" I asked.

"I know I usually just like to chat, with us being such close friends, but this time I have a few things weighing on my mind. I mean, the insurance report is not favourable. The black box reports you taking the car off auto-drive mode and purposely driving recklessly. You weren't on any drugs or mind-altering substances, were you? I mean, that could really hurt a man's life. Were you two out celebrating? A couple of professional doctors like yourselves acting in such a manner could ruin your practice."

"What practice?" I replied.

"You don't consider this nice office and all your patients a decent practice?"

"I used to," I said. "Till I realized it was all a farce. I mean, we didn't really build this, did we? We finished university, and then internships were provided for us. Our residencies were assigned to us, and then this building was assigned to us. Lastly, our patients were assigned to us. While you are running it and living the life, you can fool yourself into believing that you built it up yourself, but you didn't. The government did it all, and now it's become increasingly clear they can remove it at will."

"Semantics, Doctor," Tarleck said. "It's here. It exists. You have an exceptional life, a higher allotment than most for petrol and living accommodations. I mean, you live a pretty good life. Why mess all of that up chasing something that doesn't exist? The system is proven; it works. I don't want to see you lose it all."

"Because you care so much about us, right?" Jacob said quickly.

"Indeed I do," the inspector replied. "We're all friends here."

"And if we stop?" I said. "I mean, if we just forget these crazy notions and go back to work? What then? What of the crash?"

"What crash?" CSI Tarleck said. "Accidents happen. I'm sure that if further investigation is done, we can find a malfunctioning central control computer that caused the vehicle to act in a dangerous way, and the two occupants are free from all liability. Then all of this will fade away. Anyway, I'll leave you two to think it over. I'll see you soon."

"Jesus loves you!" I shouted.

A fairly large arm was quickly under my chin, and the harsh reality of a brick wall was against my back. "What in the world did you just say to me, you little worm?" Tarleck said. All friendliness, real or phony, was gone from his voice.

I was up to my neck in it, so I may as well go for broke. "I said that Jesus loves you," I murmured, finding it harder to say it this time with a forearm in my throat.

Tarleck said, "Now, let's be clear. Our friendship only goes so far, dear doctor. If you would like to go on breathing, do not *ever* speak to me like that again. I don't care for old, dead religions, and I don't give one tiny concern to who does or does not love me, least of all an ancient, mythical character we tossed away long ago. Are we clear?" I was terrified and didn't respond. "Are we clear, Doctor?" he repeated.

"Yes," I gargled. "Perfectly clear."

With that, he turned sharply and stepped towards the door. Then he stopped, composed himself, and turned slightly towards Jacob. "How's your hand?"

"Fine," Jacob mumbled. "A bit of a sharp pain just now, when you asked, but mostly fine."

"Good, very good." And with that, he was down the hall, slamming the office door and giving me a huge sigh of relief.

Jacob bounced up and grabbed me. "Are you all right?" he inquired.

"I'm fine."

"Are you insane?" he yelled. "Why would you say that? Why would you antagonize that man? He's scary enough when he's calm. Besides, we don't even believe in Jesus or any of that stuff!"

"Grandpa does, and I'm starting to think that if he's right about everything else, maybe he's right about this Jesus guy. You know, he told me once that a hateful bloke at his job was just as hard as Inspector Tarleck. But instead of being defensive back to the guy, Grandpa would always say, 'Jesus loves you' to him."

"And?" Jacob asked. "The man became his mate?"

"Eventually."

"Eventually?"

I shrugged. "Yeah, well, the guy did beat up Grandpa quite a few times first. These things don't resolve themselves instantly, you know."

"Oh, well, if you were looking to get beaten, keep it up. I really thought he was going to dismantle you."

"I know. I thought so too. But he didn't."

"You are aging me at an alarming rate," Jacob quipped.

"Sorry. I'm not sure where it came from. I felt I had to say it."

Just then, the door opened again. "Sorry I'm late," a female voice yelled down the corridor; it was Chloea. She was always late for one reason or another, and usually it agitated us, but not today.

"It's fine," Jacob shouted back. "We wouldn't have it any other way." He got up, walked over to me, and straightened my tie. "Pull yourself together, mate. We have patients to see."

We had to get some work done. We had been neglecting our patients, and no matter what life was giving us, our patients were always very important to us.

"We need to discuss your surgery, Jacob," I said.

"I know," he replied. "It's evident that I didn't really need surgery, so I guess we need to find out why they did it."

"And *what* they did."

CHAPTER 40

A few days passed, and Grandpa's eighty-fifth birthday was pressing closer. I couldn't help thinking that somehow this was all my fault. I knew it was a stretch to solely take the blame for the state of the entire world. I knew so much of what Grandpa said had shaped this cold, clinical, godless society happened before I was born. Still, I felt responsible. When I needed him more than ever, he was being sent away. How had we allowed him to be moved to latter care, the place people went to die? He was not even sick. We needed to do something, but what?

People weren't allowed to keep pensioners at their homes. Research showed they belonged in guarded communities, like the one he was in. *Research.* I supposed that word had lost its meaning for me. Data, research, studies – they all had new meanings now. Lies, manipulation, fraud. *What on earth do you do when you find out everyone in the world is a liar? And not only do the masses believe the lies, but they want to believe them? This is useless. I've had these thoughts a million times over the past few months. But what are we going to do about it? They run the governments, the news, the programming, the interweb – everything.*

Why did Inspector Tarleck go so insane over the name of some old, mythical character? Of course, Jesus wasn't mythical to Grandpa. I already know about Jesus and all other religions; they taught this stuff early on in schools. It was an archaic way of controlling people. These old religions imposed rules and regulations, disguised as morality, into it subjects while the ones at the top accumulated wealth and power. But Grandpa said Christianity was not that way. He said it was misused and perverted for gain, but in its purest form, it was love, decency, charity, and caring.

Tap, tap, tap. Someone was at my door.

"Oi! Lazy bugger! You planning to work today?" It was Jacob.

"Yes, sorry. I was just thinking," I replied.

"Let's go fly a kite!" he blurted out suddenly.

"now?"

"Of course not now, you benny. After work."

"Uh, okay. And where might we get a kite?" I enquired.

"Oh, we don't need a kite."

Now I was really curious. We were going to fly a kite without a kite?

The day chugged on. I had lots to do today. Mr Lathenner was complaining about his sore ankle again, and he insisted on debating my findings. He read a lot of web books, so he was quite the armchair doctor. Work was finally over after what seemed like an endless day, and we were off to fly a kite .... I think.

We arrived at a big field. "We could have just gone to the park," I said.

"Do you need your comm device to fly a kite?" Jacob asked.

"No."

"Then leave it in the car."

We got to the middle of the field. Jacob turned abruptly. "You don't just create a global epidemic, real or fake, without some sort of trail. There has to be evidence somewhere, and we need it."

"That's it? That's your big idea – get some evidence? That's brilliant, man. Why didn't I think of that? Of course! Evidence! I think I read somewhere that in court cases, they would sometimes use evidence."

"You finished yet, Mr Sarcastic?" he snapped.

"For now. But while that's bad, it's not news. We not only don't have any access to the files, but we don't have access to the places the files are stored, even if we knew which files we were looking for – which we don't."

"True, but I think the good doctor knows."

"McTarvish? Well, suppose he knows where to get evidence. Why exactly would he help us?"

"I think he wants to help. The machine he invented is being perverted into something dreadful. There is no way he likes that."

"Okay, so what? We go see him again? Because the place he works is tight on security."

"No!" David said. "I'll invite him to our office."

"And why would he come? I mean, what's his motivation to come see us? It's way out of his way."

"I don't know," Jacob said. "Why did he come to our room? I'm following a hunch."

"We'll try it. Now, can we get out of this field?"

"Sure."

We headed home, and the next morning Jacob sent the doctor a personal telecom. Then we waited. After lunch, a reply came in.

"He's coming!" Jacob shouted gleefully.

CHAPTER 41

On Friday morning, the doctor arrived. We cleared the afternoon and gave Chloea an extra long lunch. Doctor McTarvish was punctual. "Good afternoon," he said.

"I thought you weren't coming," I replied hastily.

"Nonsense. Why wouldn't I?"

"I'm not sure. I just thought you weren't."

"Well, doctors, you both signed the papers, and from what I can see, you've been somewhat behaving yourselves."

Jacob said, "Doctor, would you like to go fly a kite with us?"

McTarvish looked puzzled, but after some explaining and a car ride, we were back out in the field.

"Now, let's talk," Jacob said.

"About what?" McTarvish replied. "We're all on the same team here. We all want the same thing, don't we? World peace? World unity? World stability?"

"World control?" Jacob interjected.

"Control is such a harsh word. Isn't control a good thing? Don't you two lead very controlled, regimented lives?"

"We used to," I replied.

McTarvish shook his head. "What is the problem, gentlemen?"

"You may not show it on the outside, Doctor McTarvish, but I think you hate this. I think your machine is being misused, and I think it bothers you. There is no way it can't," I said.

"Gentlemen the world order as we know is near perfect, and

they're about to tidy up the few loose ends with this new chip and the 'cure' of the epidemic. When that happens, there's going to be very few spots near the top where everything is comfortable. I have my spot reserved, and I'm very happy about that. In order to deal with your earlier assumption, Doctors, you couldn't be more wrong. It doesn't bother me, and I couldn't be happier."

"I'm seeing that," Jacob said. "Just exactly how many comfortable spots are available at the comfy, cosy level, Doctor?"

"Jacob!" I shrieked. "What are you saying?"

"Just asking," Jacob replied. "I mean, we already signed the papers, and we were both ahead of the rest in university. Time to move up, David."

"No, Jacob. No! Just think about what you're saying."

"I am," he replied. "Time to get my piece of the pie."

"That's more like it," McTarvish said. "I could use a good doctor like you on my research team. What about you, David?"

"What about me? No thanks," I asserted. "They don't make enough soap to deal with the filth you do. And now my brother is enticed? It's sickening, just sickening."

"It's just a thought," Jacob said. "Well, I suppose you had better be going, Doctor McTarvish. I'll walk you back to your car."

Jacob escorted the doctor out of the field and to his car. Then Jacob quietly returned to the middle of the field, where I stood, amazed.

"How could you?" I exclaimed. "How could you be interested in what that man is doing? It's so wrong."

"Relax. I'm not really interested – just a passing thought," Jacob explained.

"Really? Well, what is that in your hand? Could it be Doctor McTarvish's e-card with his personal number on it?"

"He gave it to me," Jacob said defensively. "I'm not going to use it."

"Jacob, there's much more here. Grandpa hasn't begun to explain the truth to us. He has so much more to say, and we owe it to him to try to save him, to stop them from liquidating him simply because he's hit a certain age – because the evil state says he no longer has any worth. He's a human being, and he has plenty to offer. And don't forget that just a short time ago, the people that doctor works for tried to wrap us and our car around a tree!"

"I know, David," he replied. "I was only asking. I'm sorry I got you so worked up. It'll be all right."

I drove home that night feeling disheartened and very alone. A research job with Doctor McTarvish was the envy of the scientific world, but now that we'd seen behind the façade, how could Jacob entertain the thought for even a second?

CHAPTER 42

The next few days at the office were quiet, cold, and distant between Jacob and me. I thought we were closer than ever, but that dream job had created a rift.

"I'm burnt out, David," Jacob said. "Maybe it's just that I didn't have enough time after the accident to recoup. Would you cover for me for a few days? I need to rest."

"Of course I will," I replied.

I didn't get into it with him because I was too hurt. He left, and my gut felt tight and knotted. He was going to see the doctor for an interview. All that glitter had won him over, and I had no idea how to go on alone. At the beginning, I was the one who'd wanted to forget this. I was the one who would have gladly taken that job and never mentioned the incident again. Jacob was the one who'd convinced me it was wrong on principal alone, and to care, and to fight. Now he was about to walk out on it, and on me.

A few days went by, and I didn't hear from Jacob. I didn't call him, and he didn't call me. Then one morning, he was back. But this time it was clear: he was leaving. We finished the week barely speaking, and Chloea felt it too. It was awkward and uncomfortable in the office. He was going to drop the bomb; I simply didn't know when.

"David we need to talk," he said.

My heart sunk. "You're leaving."

"It's the opportunity of a lifetime. David, I have to take it," Jacob said with confidence. "You can come too, Davey. I mean, really, we can't possibly do anything about this thing – it's too big. But we can take care of ourselves and our families. Brother, if we don't, they are going to … I mean, you saw what they did to me. That was just a starter. I'm terrified, David. But we can benefit if we just play the game. It's their game and their rules, so why fight it?"

"Because it the right thing to do. Because we should. Because Grandpa would," I replied softly.

"Why, David? Why should we?"

"I don't know!" I shouted. "I don't know. But everything inside me says we should. Something is going on in me, Jacob, and I don't know what it is, but I'm tired of fighting it."

"You're a good man, David. But this is my chance, and I need to take it." And with that he was gone.

I was alone – truly alone.

CHAPTER 43

The next few weeks were dreadfully miserable, It was quiet in the office with just me and Chloea. We finished another bland day, and Chloea left. The good doctor did indeed have some kind of government pull, because Jacob's transfer was immediate. However, it seemed the government was not as quick with the process of sending me a replacement doctor. After all, this was a two-doctor facility, and I was handling all the patients alone. It was wearing on me. I had a bit of tidying up to do so, I grabbed some papers and pushed them into a drawer, where I noticed something.

Look at that. The rag that Grandpa gave us. We never looked inside. It holds all the answers to life, he said. How could that be? It's an old, rag-wrapped box. Well, let's see what it is. I began to unwrap it. It wasn't a box, but a black, leather-covered book. *Oh, it's a Bible. An archaic book of little value and little worth to anyone, except Grandpa. It held exceptional value for him. In fact, he believed it was precious. Well, after the week I've had, why not?* I began to read, and read, and read. I had always been an excellent reader.

This was the strangest book I'd ever heard of. It said that a divine being created a man and a woman and put them into a garden, and then boom – here we all were, years later. It called mistakes sin. That was a strange word. What was sin? Why did a little thing like messing with a tree get them into so much trouble? On and on I read. I couldn't put it down. Every day for what seemed like weeks, I said goodbye to Chloea, pulled out the book, and read.

So that's who Jesus is. I was amazed at how He taught and how He lived. This Jesus was different. These followers were quite different, quite extraordinary. They cared nothing for themselves. They lived for others and died for their beliefs. *Amazing. Why? Why would anyone die for something or someone? Why suffer and be crucified for a wicked world?*

I only read at the office. It wasn't hard convincing the family that it was because of the workload, because that wasn't far from the truth. Each night I lay in bed dwelling on that book, and each night it got worse. It wasn't insomnia; it was something different. It felt like a giant man was squeezing my heart. I was so dissatisfied. I wasn't restless in my life – I was restless inside deep down inside.

Weeks went by, and finally I finished. I had my answer. In order to restore what once was, to restore fallen man, this Jesus who'd died for them had also died for me. I did have a soul, and there it was, laid bare in front of me. My sins were so apparent now, so real. A man without any sin died for me – not just died, but horribly tortured. He gave his life for mine. I dropped the Bible, and it fell to the floor. I cried out to God. A few weeks ago, I didn't know He existed. Now, I cried out, and he heard me and saved me from my sin. He gave me a new heart and a new life.

Suddenly everything was clear. Everything Grandpa talked about was made so very clear. It all made sense. This time, this place, this global happening – it was all in there. I clasped the edge of the desk and pulled myself up from my knees. I felt like the weight of the world was lifted off my shoulders. I really was new. I composed myself, straightened my clothes, and reached for my key card for the office.

As I turned to leave, the interweb terminal lit up. It was a message from the United Global Authority. The gold and blue UGA flag faded, and the speaker came on. "Attention – this is not a test. This is an announcement from the United Global Authority. Due to ongoing trouble in the Middle East and the new supply shipments to Soviet Palestine, we are hereby implementing an indefinite quarantine on the nation state of Israel. There will be no traffic in or out until further notice."

Could this be true? Was everything Grandpa said true? Was this it? Was this the beginning of the great Tribulation?

To Be Continued